The prisoner
side and unle

"You've got a choice," Mack Bolan warned, closing, making target acquisition. "Don't."

Then he read the strange laughter in the man's eyes, a look that seemed to clear away all pain. Dark instinct warned the Executioner what was next, and he knew he wouldn't reach the enemy gunner in time.

The man jammed the gun in his mouth and, staring Bolan dead in the eye, pulled the trigger. A muffled crack, and the back of his head blew off.

The soldier briefly wondered about this new insanity. Capture wasn't an option—it was succeed or die. He suspected that this was only the beginning.

But the beginning of what?

MACK BOLAN ®
The Executioner

DON PENDLETON'S
THE EXECUTIONER®
EVIL REBORN

A GOLD EAGLE BOOK FROM
WORLDWIDE®

TORONTO • NEW YORK • LONDON
AMSTERDAM • PARIS • SYDNEY • HAMBURG
STOCKHOLM • ATHENS • TOKYO • MILAN
MADRID • WARSAW • BUDAPEST • AUCKLAND

First edition January 1999
ISBN 0-373-64241-5

Special thanks and acknowledgment to
Dan Schmidt for his contribution to this work.

EVIL REBORN

For we wrestle not against flesh and blood, but against principalities, against powers, against the rulers of the darkness of this world...

—Ephesians, 6:12

True evil is a multiheaded Hydra—strike a blow to cut off one head, and two others will take its place. Yet we can't back down from its relentless charge. Quit, and we will be devoured.

—Mack Bolan

THE
MACK BOLAN®
LEGEND

Nothing less than a war could have fashioned the destiny of the man called Mack Bolan. Bolan earned the Executioner title in the jungle hell of Vietnam.

But this soldier also wore another name—Sergeant Mercy. He was so tagged because of the compassion he showed to wounded comrades-in-arms and Vietnamese civilians.

Mack Bolan's second tour of duty ended prematurely when he was given emergency leave to return home and bury his family, victims of the Mob. Then he declared a one-man war against the Mafia.

He confronted the Families head-on from coast to coast, and soon a hope of victory began to appear. But Bolan had broken society's every rule. That same society started gunning for this elusive warrior—to no avail.

So Bolan was offered amnesty to work within the system against terrorism. This time, as an employee of Uncle Sam, Bolan became Colonel John Phoenix. With a command center at Stony Man Farm in Virginia, he and his new allies—Able Team and Phoenix Force—waged relentless war on a new adversary: the KGB.

But when his one true love, April Rose, died at the hands of the Soviet terror machine, Bolan severed all ties with Establishment authority.

Now, after a lengthy lone-wolf struggle and much soul-searching, the Executioner has agreed to enter an "arm's-length" alliance with his government once more, reserving the right to pursue personal missions in his Everlasting War.

The estate was an armed camp, with the grounds washed by a shroud of brilliant light. Clearly the former United States senator had turned his exclusive Long Island home into a fortress. Even the appearance of assault-rifle-toting guards roving the grounds raised grim questions in Mack Bolan's mind. The Executioner suspected there were more problems here than he had originally anticipated.

Regardless of what was going down, he had come to Southampton for answers. A trail of rumors about a conspiracy in the upper echelons of the U.S. military and intelligence communities had been started some time ago by the former New York senator. Bolan was about to put the ball in the man's court.

Closing on Charles O'Malley's home, Bolan could almost reach out and touch the fear and paranoia he found waiting for him at the front gate.

It all looked and felt wrong. Across the sprawling, manicured grounds, bathed in the glare of floodlights, he made out the shapes of a half-dozen men with slung weapons. Four smaller silhouettes quickly took form as Dobermans.

Damn strange. Armed men braced for an assault. It was the kind of security reserved for major criminals who lived in constant fear of capture or death. Certainly not what Bolan expected from a respected former U.S. senator.

If trouble showed, then Bolan had come prepared. Beneath his black topcoat he carried a Beretta 93-R in a shoulder holster. Riding his hip was a .44 Magnum Desert Eagle. And in the trunk of his Ford rental there was an Uzi submachine gun, plus an M-16 fitted with an M-203 grenade launcher. Other essentials included combat blacksuit, garrote, Ka-bar fighting knife and fragmentation and incendiary grenades.

Bolan never banked on rumors as fact. Better prepared, though, than caught sorry on fighting necessities. It wasn't so much the ex-senator, but what the man supposedly knew. And what potential enemies he had made.

It was nearly midnight when the Executioner braked at the wrought-iron gates and was met by three large, grim-faced men. As they fanned out, Bolan read military bearing all over them. Two guards reached inside their jackets where bulges indicated hardware. The third guard snapped on a flashlight and aimed the beam at Bolan's face.

Squinting away from the light, the soldier rolled down the window and growled, "I'm Belasko. Get that light out of my face."

The light died, then the gates rolled open.

The guard with the flashlight strode up to Bolan's window.

"I need to see your identification."

Bolan flashed his fake Justice Department credentials.

"You're late. We were expecting you two hours ago."

"So let's not keep the man waiting any longer."

As he raised a walkie-talkie to his lips, the guard angled toward the security booth, waving Bolan in.

Mentally the soldier spliced together what he knew about Charles O'Malley as he slowly drove up the long driveway. When in office, O'Malley had headed a select Senate committee that had uncovered a major arms-for-drugs operation in Central and South America, which was run by CIA agents and former and then-current U.S. military men. An ex-Marine, but a soldier who had never seen combat, O'Malley had apparently made a number of legitimate contacts in the intelligence world and upper echelons of the military, before and after an honorable discharge. During his two terms, he had also undoubtedly made enemies, as once respected top brass toppled under his investigation. It was a scandal that had been major news for the past year.

There was more, but Bolan would wait for his face-to-face with the man.

And it seemed O'Malley had plenty now to tell—off-the-record.

Three days earlier, O'Malley had used a liaison to contact Hal Brognola, Bolan's contact at Justice. The liaison claimed to have been a CIA case officer in Panama who helped O'Malley in his investigation. It panned out. And it was the reason Bolan was late. Earlier, the Executioner had questioned O'Malley's liaison in Manhattan. The ex-senator was desperate to talk, claiming he was afraid for his life. Brognola had arranged for both meets.

This night was a straightforward interview. Beyond that, Bolan would determine if O'Malley had anything worth pursuing.

The Executioner parked in the circular driveway behind two luxury vehicles. As he stepped out, two more guards hurried down the stone steps that led to the pil-

lared entrance of the massive Colonial-style mansion.
Each guard carried an M-16.

As they silently led him up the steps, the Executioner
searched the grounds. It was dark, silent and still out
there beyond the gazebo, the tennis court and pool to
the south. Stately maple trees loomed here and there
around the estate. The walls surrounding the grounds
were covered in ivy. If there were security cameras, they
weren't meant to be spotted by the naked eye.

All in all it was too quiet, the soldier decided, the
calm before the storm. Or was their paranoia affecting
him? Even still, the air around Bolan crackled with nervous energy. They were on high alert, poised for the
worst. But why?

"I'm going to need your weapons, sir."

Bolan looked at the guard, then removed his Desert
Eagle and Beretta. "Just make sure they don't go too
far."

"They'll be right outside Mr. O'Malley's study with
me."

Bolan handed the guard his weapons, then gave the
grounds one last hard search.

Something was definitely wrong.

THE MAN WAS clearly on edge. Bolan found himself losing patience with the former senator's strange behavior.

"If you have something to tell, let's hear it."

"You don't have all night, is that it?"

Bolan stood in front of O'Malley's massive mahogany
desk, on which was displayed a portrait of the man with
his wife and grown son and daughter. For a full half
minute, the Executioner watched the lean, white-haired,
forty-something O'Malley nervously pace behind his
desk in full glare of lamplight.

A drink in hand, a cigarette in his mouth, O'Malley walked to the study's window and pulled back the draperies. He peered outside for several long moments. Given what he'd seen so far, Bolan was tempted to tell the man to stay away from the window.

Finally O'Malley acknowledged him. "Can I offer you something to drink, Agent Belasko?"

"No, thanks."

"I see, all business. Very well. Will you have a seat?"

Bolan settled into a wing chair in front of the desk. O'Malley smoked, drank, then dropped into a leather-backed swivel chair, facing the Executioner. The ex-senator rubbed his face, taking his sweet time gathering his thoughts.

Bolan glanced around the massive study. One wall held a built-in bookcase, wet bar, giant-screen TV and stereo. Two walls were also lined with countless pictures of the senator with family, colleagues, the celebrated of the political, social and entertaining elite.

"If you feel you've received any rude treatment, I apologize."

"No need."

"I can't take any unnecessary chances."

"So I see."

"I believe I've been followed, maybe even watched for several weeks now. I'll skip the details, but knowing what I know or what someone may think I know, I believe I'm in serious trouble. I was assured by your boss you could be trusted, that you were the man to handle this."

"Just what is it I'm supposed to handle?"

O'Malley cleared his throat. "Perhaps you're aware of my investigation into illegal activities in the lower Americas."

"Guns for drugs, run by rogue Company agents and U.S. soldiers."

"Criminal actions perpetrated by our side. It goes against everything our Constitution stands for, and everything I fought for and believe in. You'll forgive me, but you don't sound terribly surprised by what I just said."

Bolan wasn't. In his War Everlasting he had seen every ilk of criminal, terrorist and traitor. It angered but didn't shock him when one of the supposed good guys jumped ship and went for himself, whether for money or for a twisted ideology.

"I need facts," Bolan said. "Not conversation."

O'Malley nodded. "I wish to God I had something concrete. I still have friends in high—and even what some may consider low—places. When they talk, I listen. I'm also realist enough to know that whatever help I received, any intelligence passing through my hands that panned out…well, those people may have had their own agendas."

"Seems to be the way it can go."

O'Malley cracked a wry grin. "The good guys don't always wear the white hats."

"Anything is possible."

O'Malley grunted. "Why is it I'm reading you as something other than what I expected?"

"Give me something, or I'm gone. First off, do you trust me?"

"I wouldn't have you here, alone with me, about to give you sensitive information, with my own life in jeopardy by persons unknown, if I didn't trust you."

"I was referring to my weapons."

"You're safe here. I have a twelve-man security force. All highly trained professionals. All former military."

"If you'd let me be the judge of that…"

O'Malley studied Bolan, then nodded. He hit an intercom on his desk and ordered the guard who had taken Bolan's weapons into the study.

When the guard entered, O'Malley directed, "Give Agent Belasko back his weapons." The guard hesitated. "Jackson, the man is with the United States Department of Justice."

Bolan took back the Desert Eagle and Beretta and holstered his weapons.

When the guard left, O'Malley continued. "Indulge me a moment. I still believe in this great country of ours, Agent Belasko, despite what I know a few bad seeds did. The basic tenets of democracy, it's what we all live for."

"Life, liberty and the pursuit of happiness."

"Precisely. What I'm about to lay in your lap is perhaps so incredible, is so repugnant to my sense of values, that not even I want to believe it."

"Believe what?"

"I'm not even sure, but it reeks of unfinished business I began. Grant you, I have more questions than answers. I'm straightforward and reliable, and I'm telling you I think my former investigation may have only touched the proverbial tip of the iceberg."

"You don't need to convince me of your good intent or strong hunches. Your record speaks for itself."

O'Malley ground out his cigarette. "My lifework is dedicated to the truth. My own personal life reflects that. Free of scandal, rumor, innuendo. Ducks in a row. Until now. Recently I've received death threats. By mail and by phone. During the past two months, several business associates and former colleagues of mine on the Hill were murdered—rather, they were executed."

"I've been briefed."

"Then you know the police and the FBI have no leads. They believe more than one killer was involved, from what I've been able to gather about the crime scenes through personal sources. They were pros, and didn't leave behind the first shred of evidence, ghosts who killed and disappeared without a trace. I've had to move my wife to a cabin upstate. The threat is real."

"I don't doubt that."

O'Malley opened a desk drawer, pulled out a large manila envelope and slid it across the desk.

"During my extensive investigation, I uncovered some things that indicate the strong possibility of a major conspiracy within our government. It's one that seems to have no beginning, no clear trail, but I believe it goes way beyond narcotics trafficking or arms dealing. The who's who, I can't be sure. Pick one. The CIA. Our military. Colombian drug lords. Disgruntled ex-KGB, holding hands with Spetsnaz. Who knows? Maybe the former KGB and elements of the Russian special forces want to throw the new Russian democracy out the window. Or a strange combination of any of the aforementioned."

O'Malley sipped his drink, then nodded at the envelope. "I call that the Hydra file. It's yours. It does name certain individuals I believe are involved in dealing or covering up...God only knows what. Proof beyond a shadow of a doubt? Negative. The players are so numerous, they come from so many backgrounds, both international and professional... What I'm saying is that it could all lead anywhere to anything. You want facts, all I can provide is a potential starting place. I sincerely hope I'm not wasting my time and yours."

"I'm listening."

"My contacts and liaisons in the intelligence community repeatedly mentioned Hydra. Who or what this Hydra really is—an organization, a code name for something—I can't say. It's all wrapped in shadows, secrets inside secrets, cover-up over cover-up, lies on top of lies.

"What I did find out was that top military brass and fat bank accounts spread clear across this planet. No one seems to know the exact source of the money or if it was meant to be used for personal wealth, or whatever illicit purposes."

"And even the guilty aren't talking."

"Right. But there's more."

"Such as?"

"Such as why one of my intelligence contacts has seen a former five-star Army general, one William McBain, in the company of a suspected Palestinian terrorist. In fact McBain was photographed sharing a fine dining experience in one of Manhattan's four-star restaurants. That was less than two days ago. The terrorist in question is Abbas 'Hannibal' Abu."

Bolan had heard of Abu. The Palestinian had never been directly linked to any particular terrorist act, but Stony Man Farm had a file on him and Bolan knew the Palestinian had been spotted in New York City. If there was some connection to anything O'Malley was telling him and Abu, Bolan intended to find out. It was another reason the soldier had come to New York.

And now O'Malley raised another ominous question. Why indeed would an ex-general be seen with a suspected terrorist?

"That file is a composite of names of probables who may have been connected to those I brought down. Now, when their assets were seized here and abroad—the cars, the boats, the homes and seven-figure bank accounts from the Bahamas to Europe to Hong Kong—I believe my investigation opened a veritable Pandora's box. Money laundering, to be sure.

"It gets uglier. Bank presidents they were dealing with in at least four different countries have recently turned up with a bullet through the brain. Some were executed while they slept. Two were sniped off as they sat in their offices. It turned out several of these bankers were in some collusion with either former KGB agents or Spetsnaz. It was verified through another CIA contact.

"Then you have money trails that appear connected to Colombian drug lords, trails that bounce all over the world but vanish into thin air as soon as our side is ready to snare them and their funds. Then I hear rumors about a web of former military honchos, from not only the United States and Russia, but also Pakistan and even North Korea, who may be sitting on an inexhaustible supply of illicit funds."

Bolan glanced at the Hydra file. With nothing but questions and no answers in sight, the only thing the soldier could do was to turn the file over to Brognola. Stony Man would take it from there.

O'Malley cleared his throat. "I sense you're frustrated, perhaps even skeptical. Well, it gets even more ominous. That file has a couple of names of former Special Forces men who seem to have disappeared off the face of the earth after what seemed sterling military careers. Just vanished. Go figure, if you can. Well, there were rumors these men resurfaced after their disappearance. Rumor. They formed on their own or in collusion with U.S. government officials, a sanctioned global operation aimed at exterminating terrorists. Now, wherever they appeared to strike like the avenging hand of God, a lot of innocent people died. My liaison gave me names, dates and places of these botched surgical strikes. It's all there. Whatever their agenda, these guys didn't give a damn who lived or died as long as they felt their targets were included in the body count. There's my biggest concern.''

"Whoever they are, if they suspect you know about them…"

"Precisely. What's to stop them from coming after me?" A pause, then he said, "Whoever opens that file, and I'm assuming it will be you…well, I'm not a man who goes after the melodramatic, but I felt compelled to leave my staple. Perhaps even my obituary.''

Bolan was reading the file when he suddenly heard the guard dogs barking. Then he saw fear shadow O'Malley's face.

Combat senses flaring, Bolan stood. The ex-senator was moving for the window when the Executioner caught the distant chatter of automatic weapons.

A moment later the glare of light from beyond the window died as the sound of shattering glass hit Bolan's senses.

"Stay away from the window!" the soldier ordered.

Abruptly the barking ended.

Then a scream of agony raked the air beyond the study.

The Executioner was up and moving for O'Malley. Clearly whatever was happening in the former senator's shadow world was storming the gates.

2

Any doubt over the threat to O'Malley's life and the dire importance of the Hydra file vanished.

Combat senses on full alert, Bolan pinned down the direction of autofire. It came from the south edge of the estate grounds, and was growing louder with each passing second. But that didn't mean much. A frontal assault could prove a diversionary tactic to allow a silent invading force to approach the estate from other points of the compass.

The Executioner had to get out of there to check things out.

Only now Bolan had the responsibility of O'Malley. No matter what, he intended to see the former senator leave the grounds unscathed. There was far more here than even O'Malley knew. After all, a well-armed assault force had come to kill the man, and apparently the invaders weren't taking prisoners. Questions would be asked later, if Bolan even got that far.

The study doors burst open behind Bolan. He already had the .44 Desert Eagle out, prepared to shout for O'Malley to hit the floor, when he turned grim attention toward the two security guards.

For a heartbeat Bolan thought they might gun him down. Then they spotted their boss, unharmed and barreling around the side of the desk. Professionals, they obviously knew if Bolan wanted to kill their boss, O'Malley would already be dead. The M-16s lowered in their hands.

"Secure the front entrance and the driveway," Bolan ordered. "Get the front gates opened! I'm taking your boss out of here."

O'Malley echoed the order when they hesitated, and the guards moved out.

Bolan grabbed the ex-senator by a shoulder and hauled him away from the desk.

"Stay low, and do exactly as I tell you."

"The file!" O'Malley cried. He broke stride to grab up the Hydra file.

"Hold that," the Executioner said. "When we reach my vehicle, we're evacuating. Nod if you copy."

The man nodded.

Outside the study, Bolan checked his rear, finding the long hallway empty, as was the spiral staircase. All fighting sounded contained at the moment to the south edge of the driveway.

On the move, the Desert Eagle low and poised to fire, Bolan took the lead through the front doors. Autofire rattled at regular intervals, to the south still, but closing. Most certainly the residents of the quiet neighborhood were wide awake by now and calling the police. Even though Bolan knew he could get Brognola to snip official red tape, the last thing he needed was a night of detainment and hardball grilling by the local law.

From his vantage point at the top of the steps, the Executioner found one guard securing position behind a black sedan. Popping up over the vehicle's hood, the guard held back on the M-16's trigger, sprayed long streams of 5.56 mm lead left to right and back. Two other guards were firing automatic weapons at the sedan's rear.

Bolan checked the maple trees to the north and the ivy-covered wall. Enough light spilled from the mansion to reveal nothing was moving in on their flank.

"Muldare!" O'Malley shouted. When he snared the attention of the man Bolan assumed was head of security, the ex-senator added, "Belasko's taking me out of here! Cover us!"

Muldare finally nodded, then said to the other two guards, "Move out! They've secured cover behind the gazebo, but they're pinned down. Now!"

Autofire intensified from the direction of the gazebo. Bolan found it a strange order for Muldare to give his men. Why have them risk their lives, charge blind across open ground, when they should provide cover fire for Bolan so he could get their boss to safety? Was it a reckless tactical decision? Inexperience? Or something else?

Firing on the run, the guards rushed from cover. A second later, one of them cried out. Bolan glimpsed the blood spraying from the man's shattered skull.

Not even flinching over the loss of his man, Muldare cracked home a fresh clip into his M-16. Turning, he met Bolan's gaze and shouted, "What are you waiting for, Belasko, the Second Coming? I've got people on their flanks and moving up their butts! It's now or never!"

Something felt wrong about the setup, but Bolan had no choice.

Bolan gave O'Malley a hard look, then growled, "Stay beside me, and don't stop running. You ready?"

The ex-senator nodded shakily, then Bolan hauled him away from the pillar. As they pounded down the steps, he shielded O'Malley from potential enemy fire. Swinging the Desert Eagle around, the Executioner took in the south grounds, searching for enemy shadows.

He found four of them, racing from the gazebo. From there, pencil-tip flames stabbed the stygian gloom. Other muzzle-flashes pierced the darkness from the south side of the mansion.

Holding back on the trigger of his assault rifle, Muldare mowed down two men with a sweeping burst of autofire. Still two more enemy gunners began to fire relentlessly at the southern edge of the building where Bolan assumed whatever was left of the security force was covered.

On the run, Bolan triggered the Desert Eagle twice, scoring chest hits that kicked two charging invaders off their feet, slamming them to the earth.

Autofire tracked Bolan, bullets zinging off stone as he raced away from the steps. Whatever moved and fired his way became fair game.

Four armed men broke from each end of the gazebo, bolting off into two-man fire teams. They blazed away with Uzi subguns as they sought cover from either the edge of the mansion or the hedges near the tennis court.

Ahead of the Executioner, hot lead was blasting out the windows around Muldare. With glass shrapnel hitting the air, Bolan, hunched low, reached the sedan. O'Malley was breathing hard, but Bolan found the man unharmed.

"Any ballpark figure on how many numbers we're facing?" Bolan asked Muldare.

The head of security shrugged. "Ten, maybe fifteen, hard to say. Bastards scaled the wall. Dropped the dogs and a few of my people before we even knew what was happening. Must've used silencers before all hell broke loose.''

"Cover me."

As Bolan gauged the distance to his rental vehicle, fifteen feet or so, a lifetime by the sound of autofire hurled their way, he took O'Malley by the shoulder. Glancing back, moving out, Bolan saw Muldare open fire.

The Executioner sprinted across the open ground and secured cover behind his car. Looking back as O'Malley stayed crouched by the driver's side, Bolan slid down to the back of his vehicle and squatted on his haunches.

The Executioner needed heavier firepower. There was no telling how much of O'Malley's twelve-man security team was still alive. But checking the sprawled figures all over the grounds, Bolan figured the enemy had shoved the odds to a one-sided fight. To stay put in the driveway meant suicide.

"You have any men left?" Bolan shouted back at Muldare, who was now backing down the sedan, triggering his M-16 in sporadic bursts.

"I think the bastards nailed them all."

"We're on our own."

Leathering the Desert Eagle, Bolan dug out the keys to the trunk. He glimpsed O'Malley grab the door handle, then saw Muldare approach the former senator. A short burst stuttered from Muldare's assault rifle, then a heavy silence settled over the grounds beyond their position. What the hell was going on? Bolan wondered. Why the sudden cease-fire?

Before Bolan could react, Muldare drew a Glock 17 and pumped a round into the back of O'Malley's head. Even as the former senator crumpled to the ground in a boneless sprawl, Muldare started to track on, but in slow motion, as brazen as hell.

The man had to have figured he'd caught a mere Justice Department agent off guard, soft from paperwork, that Bolan would hesitate out of fear and shock. But over the years, across the countless hellgrounds, the Executioner had seen and survived too much treachery. Paralysis and confusion were for dead men.

Bolan was rising, Desert Eagle drawn, his finger curling around the trigger.

A strange smile cut Muldare's lips. "You don't know how on your own—"

The Desert Eagle finished the sentence. Hand cannon booming, Bolan tunneled a gaping hole in Muldare's chest. Launched backward, the traitor checked out with a death mask of shock and horror.

Bolan heard the body crunch to the driveway, but he was already keying open the trunk, leathering the Desert Eagle. Quickly he hauled out the M-16, fed the assault rifle a 30-round magazine and chambered a round.

Peering over the trunk, Bolan observed three men, spread across the grounds in a staggered line. Strangely enough, they were holding their turf, a frozen tableau, locked in the Executioner's death sights. Then again, perhaps it wasn't so strange, he figured. They were part of the trap that Muldare had helped engineer. In addition to the former senator's death, Bolan knew they wanted the Hydra file.

No such luck if he had any say about it.

Still Bolan needed a prisoner to lead him to the next phase. He thumbed the selector for 3-round bursts. Rising, he hit the trio, left to right. They were caught off guard at first, but as the first gunner toppled, clutching his legs and screaming in agony, the other two hardmen cut loose with their Uzis.

Just one hostage was all he needed.

Braving their wild sprays of bullets, Bolan fired on. Two 3-round eruptions from his M-16 stitched the gunmen across their chests, dropped them where they stood.

Swiftly Bolan moved toward the enemy writhing on the ground. There wasn't a second to waste. In the faint glow of light from the mansion, he read the hate and agony in the man's gaze.

Somewhere in the distance, Bolan made out the faint sound of wailing sirens. Time to go.

He had a prisoner. Or so he thought.

Bolan saw the man curl up on his side, then draw a Glock from his holster.

"You've got a choice," Bolan warned, closing, drawing target acquisition. "Don't."

Then Bolan read the strange laughter in the man's eyes, a look that seemed to clear away all pain. Dark instinct warned the soldier what was next, and he knew he could never reach the enemy in time.

The man jammed the gun in his mouth and, staring Bolan dead in the eye, pulled the trigger. A muffled crack, and the back of his skull was blown off.

Briefly Bolan wondered over this new insanity. Capture wasn't an option. Whoever had sent this kill team was playing for keeps—and bigger game. Succeed or die.

The Executioner scanned the bodies. In the sheen of light, he was momentarily stunned by another puzzling sight.

Bolan moved and toed each of the first few corpses he found. The enemy wore black, with webbing fitted with commando dagger, side arm, sound suppressor and spare clips for either a Glock pistol or an Uzi submachine gun.

What aroused Bolan's curiosity was the mix of nationality. Among the dead attackers, he recognized Asians, Americans or perhaps Europeans, and figured a couple of the dead for Middle Eastern.

What was this, an international terrorist team? Some collection of mercenaries, or some other paramilitary force, with the hardmen handpicked from all over the globe?

Moments later Bolan was beside his rental vehicle. He found the Hydra file, clutched in O'Malley's bloodstained fingers. Plucking the file, the soldier got behind the wheel. With one last glance at the man who gave his life to try to unravel a trail of lies and traitors, Bolan fired up the engine.

Sirens grew closer; the cavalry was too late.

Whatever he was putting behind, the Executioner suspected the worst hadn't even started.

This was only the beginning.

But the beginning of what?

SOME THIRTY MINUTES LATER, Bolan was heading east through the dark wooded countryside of Suffolk County, his mind buzzing with a thousand questions.

Picturesque Long Island, with its white sandy beaches and quaint fishing towns, its museums and cherished abodes of the rich and famous, had been turned into a portrait of hell that night.

Checking his rearview mirror, Bolan slowed his car. There was nothing behind him, a pair of headlights ahead, closing then passing on the westbound lane.

What had O'Malley died for? Knowledge? Was it vengeance? The potential opening of that Pandora's box the man had alluded to? And Muldare. Clearly an inside job. Who was he? Why had he done it—money, or something else? Too many riddles, just like that.

Secrets inside secrets.

Who knew the truth?

Aware he had cleared the danger zone of capture by the law, Bolan pulled over. No matter what, the rental car was history. Someone could have spotted him leaving the carnage at Southampton. The next morning he could buy wheels, with cash, at a used-car lot. Until he had some answers, Bolan was planted in New York City and vicinity. At least he had an idea of how to proceed. Unless, of course, Special Agent James Rawlins, one of the late former senator's key liaisons, had been part of the deadly trap. Bolan intended to give the CIA man a thorough grilling.

He parked on the shoulder of the road. After checking for traffic and finding no headlights, Bolan took his penlight and looked at the Hydra file. Streaks of O'Malley's blood smeared the envelope. The soldier stared at the file as if it were a venomous snake, coiled to strike.

Using his combat knife, he sliced open the top edge and removed the contents.

At first he went no further than the first page. In bold red letters O'Malley had scrawled, ''Is this the beginning of the end of the free world?'' Below he had written,

Whoever reads this will know that more than likely I am dead. Should nothing come of this information, my life and my death would have meant nothing. The good men in the world may surely perish.

Hard reality had already sunk into Bolan. He was onto something. So far he had seen too much that was unexplained and unanswered to believe the former senator suffered from paranoid delusions. And O'Malley hadn't struck Bolan as a man with a death wish.

Leafing through the papers, which appeared to be mostly numbers, bank statements, names, dates and places, Bolan picked up the cellular phone. He punched in the number to Hal Brognola's twenty-four-hour line. A few rings later Bolan recognized the tired, gravelly voice of the big Fed. It sounded as if Brognola had been up all night at his office.

"Striker here. I have an urgent package, but you need to pick it up personally. And we need to talk."

"Sounds bad."

"The interview went south. You know where I'm staying."

"I'll be there ASAP."

The line went dead. The Executioner sat alone in the dark with countless grim and nagging questions.

3

Headlights stabbed at the curtain of Bolan's motel room. Already on the move, the Executioner pulled the edge back an inch. He checked the lot, his hand gripping the shoulder-holstered Beretta. Beyond his unit he saw a young couple step out of a Camaro, the man holding a bottle, the woman laughing as they made a beeline for their room. Intent, Bolan watched until they disappeared from sight and heard a door close. Nothing else moved in the lot or beyond, but he wasn't taking anything for granted.

Not after Southampton.

He gave his surroundings another hard surveillance. A diner was across the avenue, with shadows mulling in the lit windows of the all-night establishment, which was tucked close to I-78. Beyond the eatery and interstate, his gaze flickered over the grim industrial skyline of Jersey City, Hoboken, Union City. Factory stacks, refineries and a spiderweb of high-tension wires loomed along the Hudson River. Haunted by the countless unanswered questions and by what he'd seen and survived on Long Island, the scenery about his motel could have been a picture of Armageddon.

"Problem, Striker?"

Bolan let the curtain fall. He looked at Hal Brognola, who was sitting in a wooden chair beside the twin bed.

A good hour had passed since Brognola had left Newark International in a sedan rental after departing his military flight from Washington. Another thirty minutes had elapsed after Brognola made it to Bolan's room and the Executioner got the big Fed up to speed.

Now the Hydra file was open on the dresser. Brognola had scoured O'Malley's alleged incriminating evidence about a massive government conspiracy and cover-up, looking more disturbed with each dragging minute.

"After what happened tonight, Hal, I've got a bad gut feeling I'm facing nothing but problems. Problems I can't even identify."

Brognola rubbed his face. "Not to mention an endless list of questions with no answers."

"Least of all, a who's who of renegade ghosts from our own military."

Brognola tapped the folder. "A man who headed counterintelligence and counterterrorism from inside the Pentagon was seen with a known terrorist in the city the past few days..." His voice trailed off.

"There's a connection between McBain and Abu, and I intend to find out what it is," Bolan stated.

"And sever it if it's as ugly a scenario as both of us may suspect?"

"Permanent severing."

Brognola paused, searching Bolan's face. "I can see you're on edge, which is understandable. Tonight you faced down an assassin squad, hell-bent on eliminating O'Malley."

"It was an inside job, beginning to end."

"You said the head of security was named Muldare?" Brognola asked.

"Former military, from what O'Malley said."

"Okay, well, the FBI will work with us on the crime

scene out there. I'll run down this Muldare's background. It might take a little time, but I'll get the identities and background on the others on the senator's security detail, also.''

"It's a place to start. At this point, I don't have much else.''

"What about O'Malley's liaison, this Rawlins?''

"As soon as you leave for the airport, he's first on my shopping list. He was the one who came to us, after all.''

"Using another liaison. This whole thing feels bad, Striker. I'm already looking at shadows within shadows, puzzles inside puzzles. I would watch your back, and trust no one.''

"If there's some conspiracy—and I believe there is one—I'm on my own. O'Malley's original investigation only scratched the surface.''

"I agree,'' Brognola replied. "In the event your rental was spotted, you run me back to Newark, take my wheels. Leave your vehicle here, and I'll send a man up from the Farm before dawn to take care of it. Beyond that, you've got the usual carte blanche. If official toes need stepping on, I'll be there with one phone call.''

"I won't get bogged down by our own side. I need to move, fast and hard, on this one. I need answers before the sun rises.''

"I have to concur that you may have nothing but problems on this one, Striker. At first glance at O'Malley's file, I think we've hit the mother lode.''

"But of what?''

"That's the million-dollar question—or I should say the billion-dollar question, from what I see of these bank statements, and I can't even say just how much money I'm looking at here. These figures are mind-boggling.

I'm looking at transfers of huge sums of money to Panama. Then to and from the Bahamas. To and from Paris, to and from twelve other countries. I'm no accountant, but I daresay these figures equal the GNP of a lot of Third World countries."

"It has to be more than narcotics or arms smuggling, Hal."

"Shipments of nuclear materials?"

"I don't know for certain. But my hunch is we need to be looking for the source of the money and why all this juggling of these sums to all these countries. Someone, or some organization, is setting up an agenda."

"Whatever is happening, I've got in front of me an impressive list of players the late ex-senator left behind. First, and most disturbing, of course, a former five-star general, schmoozing with a known terrorist who is believed to be bankrolled by certain fringe elements of the old-line guard of Russia. Bank presidents in a dozen countries, with half of those countries not exactly what I'd consider friendlies. Pakistani military brass, names of German businessmen, more bankers, a North Korean colonel, names of what O'Malley grouped as former KGB and Spetsnaz. American Special Forces. Names and dates of terrorist attacks in six different countries, supposedly done in the past two years by conspirators on our team. Somehow, we're supposed to believe, it's all linked."

"O'Malley believed it."

"And died for it. And that fact alone has made me a believer."

"Definitely an ugly list of players, with our own military thrown onto the plate."

Brognola looked at Bolan. "Some U.S. government

conspiracy that reaches around the globe, is that your hunch?''

"I don't think O'Malley was one for melodrama. Read that inscription of his, and I have to believe the man knew he wasn't long for this world."

"Only he didn't know who might be coming for him."

Bolan took a chair beside Brognola. "Or why exactly."

Brognola stared at the file. "O'Malley nailed some people who deserved nailing. He was a stand-up politician, no skeletons in his closet, no agenda, at least not that I'm aware of. I know his track record, and I strongly believe we've got something here. Only question, again, is what? And why? And who?''

Brognola fell silent, grim. Looking down at the Hydra file, he said, "I'll get this to Aaron ASAP and turn him loose on it. He'll have something for you in the morning. If nothing else, he'll have a place for you to start, some location of a target on this file. If these names on this list can be tracked down, you may have yourself quite a grim chore ahead of you, Striker. Some of this will be easy enough to check out, but some of it will take time. I can't even promise Bear can put a track on some of our own on this list who have supposedly vanished into thin air or gone to ground and are operating…God only knows what."

If anyone could get the ball rolling in the right direction, Bolan knew Aaron "Bear" Kurtzman, Stony Man Farm's resident computer expert, was the man for the job.

"I'll call you first thing in the morning," Bolan said, slipping into his overcoat.

"The Farm or my office. I have a feeling I won't see

a good night's sleep until this thing—whatever it is—is tracked down, rooted out.'' Brognola stared at his old friend for a long moment, his eyes full of concern. "Good luck, Mack. Be careful.''

Bolan nodded. Both men understood, of course, the perils of any mission the Executioner undertook. At any time an enemy bullet, knife or bomb could take him out. They understood the ultimate price could be paid in an instant, but they freely, even gladly accepted the risks. In a world that every day seemed to grow more insane with greed, violence and treachery, both men knew all that kept it from devouring the human race was a few good people.

After the solemn pause, Bolan said, "I'll be in touch.''

Brognola looked weary, the weight of the world on his shoulders as he picked up the Hydra file and stood. "Take care, my friend, and good hunting. My gut is churning and telling me you won't even know who the good guys are on this one—let's just hope you don't find who's who until it's too late.''

The Executioner was grimly aware of just how true that was as he opened the door and led Brognola into the night.

THERE WAS A PROBLEM. Perhaps the whole hit had been a total fiasco, but from the beginning he had expected as much.

Standing on the deck, amidships, Ben Calhoun stared at the dark and distant shoreline of Long Island. His mind was still sifting through the contingency plan in the event the mission here had gone south.

Gut instinct told him the strike team wasn't returning. Already he'd given the order, heard the diesel engines throbbing to life as the cabin cruiser began to head out to sea.

He checked the illuminated dial of his chronometer. No radio call, and they had been gone for almost four hours. Everything had been planned down to the smallest detail, and even total annihilation of the squad, either by the police or their own hand, didn't necessarily signal failure.

Even then he could hear the two Hueys flying back to the freighter, bound for Paris. Only moments ago the pilots had received their orders. The rubber outboards that had carried the team to the vans would, of course, be left on shore. The rental vans couldn't be traced to him, either. But that was how it was all planned anyway: phony paperwork, false ID, a slew of false passports and changed identities and rearranged histories. As far as anyone knew, especially the United States military, they were all dead. Gone, ghosts vanishing, no trace.

Folding his hands behind his back, Calhoun smiled, his narrowed gaze fixed on the blinking eye of the shrinking lighthouse.

It had all been set in motion, five years and six months ago to that night. So long ago, he only had vague recollections of its genesis. Ghosts of memories darted through his mind. They had been drawn from various intelligence agencies, numerous military brass from the elite of special forces from four different countries. The biggest of the major narcotics traffickers, arms dealers, terrorist leaders, warlords and dictators had been brought together by an offer they couldn't refuse.

Was it possible? Of course it was, he knew.

The offer was so incredible, but with an agenda that could be attained with clearly defined goals there for the taking, that it could change the destiny of the entire world.

The project was code-named Hydra.

Even then, he shoved it all to the back of his mind. It was a mammoth undertaking, but it was already in motion. Once started, there was no turning back.

And it had already begun.

Breathing in the salt air, he shivered a little beneath his black bomber jacket. He wasn't quite six feet tall, lean as a whip, with a hawkish face and short-cropped iron gray hair and slate gray eyes. It wasn't much in terms of size, but Calhoun was one of the most dangerous men in the world, whether armed or unarmed. Created and trained by his own government, now he was part of something that would be the single greatest coup in human history. Soon, very soon, he would be a giant, a god, and they would tremble from the four corners of the earth.

The sound of the rotor blades was swallowed by distance, the bulky shadows of the gunships vanishing in the black sky and infinite expanse of the Atlantic Ocean.

"You are leaving them?"

Former Special Forces Major Calhoun felt the presence of the Palestinian. He didn't need to look to know the man was there. Aura—it was all in the energy. Reading men, knowing their motivations and the limits of their abilities was what made Calhoun think he was the only one to lead the project.

Turning his head, Calhoun peered at the short, stocky figure. With long black hair and a thick beard, Abbas "Hannibal" Abu looked more like a fugitive on the run than one of the world's foremost terrorists who had more money, contacts and connections than most intelligence agencies.

"They were told to contact us at exactly 0100. Since they haven't, I'm left to assume they're dead."

"And if their mission was not successful? I have lost several good men, Major."

Calhoun clenched his jaw. "Let's get an understanding between us, Abu. Every man knew and accepted, knows and accepts the risks going in. Capture is unacceptable. No matter what, the mission has succeeded because I had my own people on the inside from the beginning. The cause of the Coalition is greater than any of us. What we have embarked on is the real and only true holy war."

Abu frowned, but lost the expression in the next moment. "You think this…ex-senator could have possibly known something?"

Calhoun felt a tight smile ghost his lips. The Palestinian worried too much, but telling him that would only reinforce his anxiety. It was best to say as little as possible. Hatred first, then greed drove the Palestinian. Abu had very little self-control. But he was a terrorist, not a soldier, much less a disciplined fighting machine.

"I wanted the man dead, mister," Calhoun said, "for what he did to a number of good friends and soldiers I knew."

"Vengeance. I understand that."

"Then let it go at that. Now," Calhoun said, putting a hard stare on the man, "my problem is your people having our merchandise ready for tomorrow."

"They will have it."

"I hope so. This has come too far for any setbacks or snafus. And your man is ready to go at 0900?"

"He is. It is something we both arranged months back."

"The other thing?"

"Film at eleven, as you Americans would say."

"No. It better be in living color for my eyes only, Abu. Both."

"But of course you will see it with your own eyes."

"I suggest you get some sleep. Tomorrow you people are getting your big shot."

The man's dark eyes peered at Calhoun. "Big shot?"

"For your own vengeance against the Great Satan."

Now the Palestinian smiled, even chuckled.

Calhoun looked away, watching the winking lighthouse slowly fade as the cruiser pushed farther south.

"I'm glad you and I have the same hatred for your country," Abu said. "It keeps us together and strong in this. We will succeed."

Calhoun grunted. "Whatever. Now, if you'll excuse me, all this understanding and 'we shall overcome' routine may make me break out in tears. You don't want to see a grown man cry, do you?"

Out of the corner of his eye, Calhoun saw the Palestinian scowl at the tone of bitter sarcasm. As the man walked away, Calhoun shook his head softly. There was a lot the Palestinian didn't understand, much less know. At the moment, Abu was useful to further the ultimate goal of the Coalition. One pawn, yes, in a game where the stakes involved the human race.

IT WAS ONE of those brick tenement dwellings that had become anonymous landmarks in the run-down sections of New York City. For whatever reasons, the Company liaison had chosen the Lower East Side to hole up. In this neighborhood of derelicts, crack addicts and drug dealers, it would be a stretch to call the agent's place a safehouse.

As luck would have it, Bolan had found a spot to park

his new rental car on the street. With typical good planning, Brognola had brought an alarm system for Bolan to hook up to the sedan. There was no telling where the mission would take him, but since Bolan couldn't very well carry around his armament and gear at all times, any would-be car thief would be hit with a screeching alarm that could alert the five burroughs. Bolan hoped it didn't come to that; he didn't need any attention from NYPD.

Checking for any shadows of potentially dangerous denizens of the night, Bolan moved up the trash-littered steps. He walked past a wino, who was passed out. Moments later he entered the building and reached the appointed door.

Earlier he had met the man in a bar in Manhattan, the arrangements thanks to Brognola. Information had been passed on to Bolan about the late ex-senator, allusions to conspiracies and cover-ups, all manner of grim subterfuge happening within the hallowed hallways inside the Beltway.

The time for games and theories was over. Bolan wanted precise answers to a slew of bad questions.

He rapped on the door, hearing scuffling, he believed, from inside. Then silence. As he checked the hallway with its cracked walls and lone rat skittering across the floor, the door was suddenly opened and the ugly snout of a handgun was thrust toward his face.

4

Bolan reacted with lightning speed, grabbing the gun hand just as it cracked a round.

Angry force surged back at Bolan. Grappling with the faceless shadow in the inky murk of the doorway, the soldier couldn't tell right off if it was the Company man or not. Given his night already, the Executioner wasn't taking any chances, but he wasn't looking to apply lethal force—unless necessary. Dead men couldn't talk. And instinct told Bolan whoever he faced was most likely surprised by his arrival, and scared of something or someone.

Bolan blocked the left hook. As the shadow grunted and strained, the Executioner caught a whiff of liquor and the smell of fear. Exploding forward, Bolan slammed the body against the wall. In the frenzy of movement the soldier still couldn't clearly see the shadow as they tumbled, locked together.

Hammering the gun hand off the wall and sending the weapon flying, Bolan twisted, hurled his weight into his adversary's chest. As the shadow burped air from starved lungs, Bolan bent at the knees, gripped an arm and flipped the figure over his head. The man crashed to the floor.

Blood racing, the Executioner strode into the room, the Beretta whipped out of its holster.

"Belasko?"

Bolan loomed over the outstretched figure of Special Agent James Rawlins.

"Stay down," the Executioner ordered, taking in the Spartan living room, listening for the slightest noise from any other surprise guests.

No sound, except the rattle of distant gunfire, a wail of a siren from somewhere blocks away. Bolan patted Rawlins down roughly.

"You mind telling me what the hell is going on?"

Bolan glanced at the man's scowl. Pain was etched on the long, square-jawed face, which was framed by a scraggly mop of salt-and-pepper hair. The man was long and lean, dressed in a black turtleneck, jeans and dark desert boots. With his hair and goatee, Rawlins looked more like a hand-to-mouth painter in the park than a Company operative.

"Exactly my first question to you," Bolan answered as he dug a Colt .380 pistol out of the agent's ankle holster, then seized a commando dagger sheathed on his other ankle. After dropping both weapons in the pockets of his coat, Bolan took the discarded Glock 17 and tucked it in his waistband. He gave the shabby apartment a quick but thorough search, keeping one eye on Rawlins the whole time. He stood in the doorway of the lone bedroom, flicked on a light, then crouched low, Beretta poised. There was nothing but a twin bed and nightstand in the sleeping cubicle.

"I'm alone, Belasko. Skip the storm-trooper act."

"It's no act." Bolan checked the hall, found it deserted, then shut the door. He fixed grim attention on Rawlins. "You always greet a contact with a gun in his face?"

"I think I was followed," Rawlins said, groaning as he rubbed his back, slid up on a knee.

"By who?"

"I don't know who."

"Where were you? Say around midnight."

"I was out on a surveillance. And do you always bust up your contacts, then ask questions later?"

"I've had a tough night."

"Likewise. I'm jacked up on a fair amount of paranoia, Belasko, and I couldn't see your face through the peephole. I didn't know who you were. Besides, the gun wouldn't have gone off if you hadn't grabbed it."

"Like I said."

"Right. Tough night. And what do you mean where was I at midnight?"

"That gunfire draw attention to this place?"

"In this part of town, if the natives don't hear gunfire they get nervous. It's why I chose this hellhole. Low profile."

Bolan could tell this interrogation wasn't going to be easy. Pinning Rawlins with a cold stare, he said, "O'Malley's dead."

"What?"

Was it genuine confusion or an act? Bolan wondered.

"He was hit tonight—midnight, give or take. His estate was stormed by what I can only call a multinational assassin squad that was under orders to kill the former senator. Even if it meant committing suicide in the event the team was cornered or captured."

"Really?"

Bolan kept his penetrating stare on Rawlins. "It was an inside job."

"That a fact?"

"You don't sound too surprised. Tell me why that's making me a little nervous."

"They're here."

Grim, Rawlins stood and walked to the lone iron-barred window. There, he pulled back the curtain and stared outside for long moments.

"Who is 'they'?" Bolan growled.

"I don't know."

"Don't jerk me around, Rawlins."

Rawlins dropped the curtain and faced Bolan. "What I meant to say is I don't know who exactly they are." He rubbed his face, his Adam's apple bobbing as he swallowed hard. "Listen, you mind if we sit down? I could use a drink. There's a few serious items we need to go over."

Bolan saw the bottle and glass on the kitchen counter, which was littered with fast-food wrappers and an empty pizza box.

"I couldn't agree more," Bolan said. "Skip me on the cocktail, but keep your hands in sight. Now, my questions to you should be obvious."

The soldier holstered the Beretta and took a seat on the small couch. He watched as Rawlins filled his glass, drained half, then lighted a cigarette with a trembling hand. A solemn, distant gaze shadowed the agent's features, as if the man were haunted by memories or knowledge he wished he didn't possess.

"By that," Rawlins said, "I assume you mean if I was part of the setup."

A pause.

"I'm waiting," Bolan said.

"No. Take it or leave it. No."

Bolan nodded. "For the moment I'll take it."

There was another long moment of silence, as the

agent gathered himself, then seemed to retreat. "Let me ask you something, Belasko. What do you think is the most important thing in the world to men of power?"

"More power."

"Yes and no. Information, Belasko, information equals knowledge, and knowledge keeps one side one up on the other."

"What sides are we talking about?"

Rawlins dropped in an easy chair, facing Bolan. "The hell of it is, I don't even know who's on what side anymore. I honest to God have nothing but hunches and guesses as to whatever knowledge I may or may not possess."

"I don't have time for mysteries. O'Malley's dead, I have what he called the Hydra file, complete with supposedly a lot of intelligence gathering you did for him and dropped off in his lap."

Rawlins grunted. "The Hydra file, huh?"

"Is Hydra some organization? A code name for some conspiracy O'Malley was about to smell out?"

Rawlins stared into his drink, then looked at Bolan. "I don't know who or what Hydra is. I do know that word has turned up over the past couple of years from informants and sources I've used. If they used it, it was because they were beginning to gather bits and snatches of the puzzle we now face. Once they used the word, I never saw them again."

"Rawlins, I don't dance well."

"Hey, listen to me, okay? I had close contacts established in many countries, men I could trust. There were times I knew I was onto something, I knew they were onto something. Unfortunately it would appear if they dug beneath the surface, well, they turned up dead or just vanished."

"But the surface of what?"

"I can't be sure. First of all, before you blast off and lose all patience with me, O'Malley didn't have squat without me. I put him in the game."

"The man wasn't looking to be a star on the morning talk shows."

"Nor am I."

"This was no game to O'Malley."

"Nor I. I met the man in one of those fancy restaurants where all the lobbyists, the newshounds and Hill crusaders gather in Washington. A drink here, some schmooze there, sensing the man may or may not be straight up—well, I fed him a few bones."

"So, you had an agenda."

"To keep on living, that was my agenda and still is." He smoked with a nervous fury. "And, I now believe, that agenda is to try to stop what I fear may be the beginning of the biggest criminal endeavor the world has ever known."

"I need facts, names, not Armageddon paranoia."

Rawlins scoffed. "I know enough to realize that as we near the turn of the century, the face of the world as we know it now may change forever. You know how much this government knows, has done and won't tell its people because, again, knowledge is power." He tapped the side of his head. "Not true with someone who has seen it. Now, I don't need files, computer disks, fax machines, diaries or film at eleven. It's all here, in my mind. Let me tell you, Belasko, the world *is* changing as we speak, and it isn't for the better."

"The more something changes..."

"Yes and no." Rawlins drew deep on his cigarette, exhaled a cloud that nearly cloaked his face. "The only constant is human nature, and I think that whatever conspiracy may be happening in this country and beyond, under our very noses, is human nature taken to the extreme.''

''You're talking in riddles.''

''And you're being kind by not telling me I'm full of crap.''

''You're right, I'm losing patience.''

Rawlins took a manila envelope from the nightstand and pitched it onto the couch beside Bolan.

''In there is a small piece of the puzzle. Thing is, Belasko, I've only been throwing questions out there. I want answers myself, but the more I see, the more I'm left groping around in the dark.'' He stubbed out his cigarette and fired up another. ''Now, what do we know? O'Malley brought down a few, shall we say, boys in the know and with major clout who were supposed to be on the home team. That was only round one. O'Malley died because of round one and because he was stepping into the ring for round two. The man knew the risks, we talked about them, at length.''

Rawlins melted into a dark and brooding figure, looking almost ghoulish to Bolan in the soft lamplight. ''I've been a case officer all over the lower Americas, the Middle East, Asia. I've also done freelance work for the Company. Meaning paramilitary operations, even wet work for the CIA's secret special-operations division, which really isn't so secret. I've done and seen many things I'm not real proud of. Whether you want to believe it or not, I know for a fact that our nation's economy is fast approaching a life-and-death struggle, simply because it's pitted against the major criminals on this planet who have more, own more and control more than most governments. Drugs and guns, the import and export of them, is fast going to replace oil, textiles and whatever other legitimate free enterprise to make a buck in the country. That, my friend, is the proverbial tip of the iceberg regarding what you saw tonight. And it's those who can do something to stop it who are the ones who not only 'created' but who are fomenting and profiting from the chaos and mayhem you see in America.''

''I've heard this argument before. I've seen men profit, too, from the blood of others. In war and in civilian life. It's the way of the savage.''

''You don't sound convinced.''

''There's bad seed to be found anywhere. Doesn't mean the whole crop is rotten.''

''Spoken like one who still believes in his fellow man.''

''Where there's life, there's hope.''

Rawlins seemed to mull something over. ''One thing I do know is that it's a free-for-all out there, for anyone with a little power, a little knowledge, for anyone with the guns and the determination to use all the aforementioned. Belasko, unless you've been living in a bubble the past twenty years, and I'm sure you haven't, the world and its resources are shrinking every day as the human race overruns the planet. In twenty years they say the world's population will be in the double-digit billions.

''What I'm saying is a few, an elite few, have maybe formed or are establishing a criminal enterprise that may be hell-bent on grabbing up what's left before it's all gone. I've been on this thing for over a year. I've tracked outrageous bank accounts, ID'd men of power and prestige from our country in the presence of some of the world's most notorious drug traffickers and terrorists.

''What will happen, do you think, in a world where a core of haves use a world of have-nots as slaves or worse. Something is happening out there, and there's a reason why the criminal elite of the planet is globe-trotting with a top member of the Pentagon brass. Who knows? There may even be a large number of more guilty people on our side. Conspiracies in our military and government? Greedy and ambitious men taking what they want? Guns for drugs? Arms for hostages? Assassinating our own presidents? I'm sure none of this comes as any great surprise.''

Finally Bolan opened the envelope and pulled out the 8×11 pictures. On top of the short stack was a wide, bulldog face with mean eyes, rigid in expression. Bulldog was drawing on a cigar and locking gazes with a swarthy, bearded man. It looked to be a restaurant setting, with two other Middle Eastern men in expensive jackets in the background. Bolan thumbed through the photos.

"The top one was McBain?"

Rawlins grunted. "And Abu. We discussed them briefly when we first met. But those are only a few of the pictures me and my surveillance team has managed, and in just the past few days.''

"How many men do you have working for you?"

"Two.''

Bolan's gaze narrowed. "Just who are you working for?''

"The Company—or a fringe element of it. Back to my surveillance photos. Five down, you'll find a former Special Forces major by the name of Ben Calhoun. Three tours of duty in Nam, and the guy's decorated out the wazoo. Rumors say he did some nasty things over there for the home team. Career military, or so it seemed. Thing is, no one's seen or heard from the man in six years. Nor has anyone heard of, or from, the surviving soldiers in his Special Forces group. That was until about nine months ago. Calhoun was sighted in Beirut after a disastrous commando raid on a terrorist stronghold. Happened in the heart of the city, and it looks like Calhoun was either sanctioned or hired out as an avenging angel. He and his people got trigger-happy, left about twenty to thirty civilian casualties, including women and children. That's where a case officer caught that shot of Calhoun. A week later he was sighted in Tel Aviv, with McBain.''

"That's enough for the rumors about a secret counterterrorist unit with ties to one William McBain?''

"It was certainly a beginning. So I dug into McBain's closet for any rattling skeletons I could find. Using the wonders of modern computer technology and some other methods we apply, I tapped into McBain's bank accounts in three different countries.''

"Let me guess. The man's a millionaire.''

"Ten, maybe more times over. Man was the big shot of the big shots at the Pentagon, but his salary would hardly equal the figures I uncovered. His specialty was counterintelligence, counterterrorism. He retired six years ago, and he's a widower. No one seems to know what the man has been doing these past few golden years of his. We found out he has several homes—one in Cartagena and a château in the French Pyrenees, and a case officer in the Philippines claims the former general even owns an entire floor in an exclusive hotel in Manila. Picture getting pretty ugly?

"Okay, let me darken things a little more. I've got Colombian diplomats caught in the company of two suspected major Cali traffickers, right here in New York. I've got a German businessman, Max Tielig, seen schmoozing with the dips and the traffickers. Tielig deals in diamonds and also the export of industrial machinery—primarily to South America. I'm sure you can figure some of the connections there. Bottom line, I've got all these players, sighted together, as recently as yesterday.''

"I need a starting place, Rawlins."

"How about a safehouse for Abu and his brother terrorists? I had them staked out tonight. That's where I was."

"Where?"

"The Bronx, and they're armed to the teeth. I also made them stockpiling brown crates in a warehouse near the river. A crew of Abu's cronies guarding said warehouse with AK-47s. One of them dropped a crate, and out pops an RPG-7."

Bolan looked Rawlins dead in the eye. He wasn't about to trust Rawlins at his word. But something secret and deadly was taking place. The soldier need look no further than what had happened to O'Malley that night.

"Now the grabber, Belasko. I've got a man deep inside the German-Colombian circle. On the surface he hints it's about guns and drugs and the shipping of the necessary chemicals used for producing cocaine. But he thinks something else far worse is going on."

When Rawlins fell silent, Bolan flipped the photos on the couch and said, "How come I get the feeling you're holding back?"

"You know pretty much all I do. Can I make a suggestion?"

"I'm listening."

"Why don't we go pay Abu's boys a Bronx visit. Who knows—we shake some trees, snakes may fall out."

It made sense to Bolan. Time was wasting. The best

way, he knew, to get some concrete answers was to go to the source. Or rather, he was grimly aware, one of the sources.

Still, he had to start someplace.

Bolan stood. He dropped the Company agent's weapons on the couch.

"Gesture mean you trust me now?"

Bolan put an edge in his voice. "You sought us out, Rawlins."

"At O'Malley's insistence."

"Whatever. Clearly it's hit the fan. I'm here. I don't see where I have a choice."

"There's always a choice."

"So, don't give me a reason to make the choice for you."

"Belasko," Rawlins said, rising, then retrieving his weapons, "in the short time I've known you...well, it was O'Malley's idea to go to the Justice Department. He didn't trust anybody else. Looking at you, I get the feeling you're no Justice Department issue. Since you asked me the same thing, mind if I ask, just who and what you are?"

Bolan slowly moved for the door. "Let's just say, in a perfect world you wouldn't need me."

5

With no choice but to take both the mission and the mystery as it unfolded, Bolan rode through the night with his new ally. Dawn was still a few hours away.

Having taken the sedan rental, Bolan had Rawlins drive. Up FDR Drive to the Cross-Bronx Expressway, they had ridden in tight silence. With little traffic, they made the target warehouse in short order. North of the warehouse district, the frame houses, tenements, closed shops and shopping marts of the Bronx stretched away in the dead of the night.

Slowly Rawlins made his way down a narrow, trash-littered alley where unlit, two-story buildings loomed on either side.

Bolan kept one eye on the Company man while surveying his surroundings. If Rawlins was leading him into a trap, Bolan wouldn't hesitate to make the man pay the ultimate price. After all, the soldier had nothing but a handful of mystery. And trusting anyone now on his word could prove foolish—and fatal.

"We close?" Bolan asked.

Rawlins rounded the corner of the last building and rolled across a short dark stretch of paved no-man's-land. Beyond a row of trash bins, Bolan spotted a chain-link fence. A dozen yards or so inside the fence, he saw forklifts, two tractor trailers and a dark, empty guard booth. Both machinery and the 18-wheelers were parked at the edge of a wide lot, near a two-story warehouse.

Rawlins pulled in behind a garbage bin. "We're there. It may look empty, but I've had this place staked out the last six nights. If I'm not here, my people have it spied. One guard, armed, patrols the grounds every thirty minutes."

Bolan stepped out. Nothing moved in the alley behind. Looking around the bin, he gave the warehouse and its grounds a harder search. It was then he saw a shadow in the distance. Intently, hidden from the guard's view behind the bin, Bolan watched. He believed he made out the muzzle of an assault rifle slung across a shoulder of the shadow. But not enough light spilled from the warehouse for him to be certain.

A door opened just beyond the loading bays, and the shadow disappeared through the opening. Poor lighting could work to a silent invader's advantage, Bolan knew.

"What do you know about the perimeter?"

"Fence isn't electrified, if that's what you mean," Rawlins answered. "As for motion detectors, hidden cameras, I don't think so, but I don't know for sure. I've spotted four vehicles on any given night. Luxury cars. They come in and park on the other side. Enough to hold twelve men in all, give or take. They keep a crew here around the clock."

"How long have you known about this place?"

A mean glint lit the agent's eyes for a moment. "Since I found out they warehoused industrial machinery. Imported from Germany, no less. That was two months ago."

Bolan stared at Rawlins. "Tielig owns this warehouse?"

"No. On paper it's a front man, Alex Widerman—

whoever that is. From what I know of him, Tielig's not one to get his hands dirty.''

More riddles, Bolan thought. The list of a mixed bag of deadly players kept growing, with no end in sight, and he still had no firm confirmation as to their agenda. Well, the soldier determined, if they stored weapons here, they were most likely destined to fall into the hands of terrorists or other criminals. It was as good a place as any to launch an all-out blitz.

"Anything else you've neglected to tell me?" Bolan added.

"That detail slipped my mind."

"Abu ever make an appearance here?" Bolan asked, deciding not to push the lame excuse.

"One time, two nights ago. A truck pulled in. Looked like he was here to supervise, probably check the merchandise once it was inside. It's safe to say there's a connection between Tielig and Abu."

"Obviously. But why?"

"Tielig's a businessman. On paper it appears business hasn't been so good for him the past couple of years. Big market for weapons out there."

"Give me the keys," Bolan ordered.

"What's the plan?"

"I'm going in."

"Alone?"

"Alone."

"You realize if you even get inside, you may be facing down ten, maybe twelve heavily armed terrorists?"

Bolan took the keys from Rawlins, then went to open the trunk. "If it sounds like I need backup, you'll know."

"How?"

Bolan hauled out the M-16 with attached M-203 grenade launcher. "Gunfire."

Rawlins shook his head. Something cold and deadly seemed to shadow the agent's face.

"Belasko, I thought we'd gotten past this uncomfortable get-to-know-you phase."

Bolan cracked a 30-round clip into the M-16, then chambered a round. He shed his coat and tossed it in the trunk. There was a chilly bite to the air, but adrenaline would soon warm his blood.

"Too many unanswered questions, Rawlins."

"What are you going to do, bulldoze your way in and start slapping people around? Blow the place up? If there's explosives in there, you realize a firefight could leave that place nothing but one big smoking hole in the earth?"

"I'm aware of that."

"But it's a chance you'll take."

Bolan picked up a small satchel and filled it with spare clips for the M-16, then took a battery-powered vibrating lock pick from a duffel bag and placed it inside. Then he dropped in three thermite grenades before loading the M-203 with a 40 mm grenade. Two more grenades for the M-203 went into the satchel, then Bolan closed the zipper and hung the bag around his shoulder.

"All right, Belasko, suit yourself, be a cowboy."

Bolan shut the trunk, took out his Beretta 93-R and threaded on the sound suppressor. He tossed the keys to Rawlins.

"I trust you'll be here when I return."

"If you return."

"The way it's falling already, the only way to get some answers on this one," the soldier told Rawlins, "is to start as the hunter, then become the hunted."

"Maybe you don't get it. The moment I contacted your people and handed you O'Malley, you were already the hunted."

Bolan stared at Rawlins, then moved past the man. For some reason, Bolan strongly believed that cryptic remark. The only question was who exactly was hunting him.

After he was finished here, he suspected he might soon know who was who and what was what.

SWIFT, SOUNDLESS and alert for any movement from the warehouse, Bolan scaled the ten-foot fence and dropped to the other side with catlike grace. Beretta out and fanning the gloom, the soldier dashed across the lot. Reaching the west edge, he hugged the corner as he searched the loading dock and the door where the shadow had vanished. So far so good.

Checking his back, he found Rawlins would keep.

On his left flank, Bolan discovered a side door.

The Executioner's goal here was clear but far from simple: get in, determine who and what was inside, if possible; check whatever crates he could; hopefully eavesdrop on any conversation that might clearly identify who or what he was up against.

Either way, there was little doubt in Bolan's mind the warehouse was a weapons depot and perhaps even a command center for staging terrorist acts. For that matter, he wasn't just banking on Rawlins's word. Men toting assault rifles wouldn't be guarding a place that housed simple industrial machinery.

Thoughts of the suicide attack rose into Bolan's mind. The men inside would guard this place and its property with their lives. No doubt he was stepping into a nest of human vipers.

Thirty seconds later he had the lock picked. Quietly he opened the door and slipped inside. He left the door slightly ajar, in case Rawlins needed to make an emergency entrance, which was risky, he knew, if someone was patrolling the grounds and found the door open. Again Bolan found himself with a no-choice situation.

Snapping on a penlight, he discovered he was in a small office. His M-16 slung across his shoulder, Bolan drew the Beretta. Crouched, he shone the light on a narrow, dark hallway and spotted a thin beam of light coming, he assumed, from somewhere in the warehouse proper. He shut off the penlight and padded into the hall. Keeping his gaze fixed on the light, he looked for any shadows that might move into the soft glow.

Combat senses on full alert, he began to make out low voices. At the end of the hall, he stopped, listened. Men were speaking in Arabic, and even with his limited knowledge of the language, he could make out some of what they were saying.

"Abdul, that was too quick. You walk the entire grounds?"

"Of course. It's the dead of night, Hamil. The whole city is asleep at this hour. As we should be."

"Hardly true, my brother. Who can sleep on the eve of what could be our greatest attack yet on the Great Satan?"

Bolan felt his blood race. Both the words and the venomous hate he heard confirmed he was about to strike the mother lode.

Peering around the corner, he found stacks of wooden crates, piled five or six high. At first glance he believed there were many dozens of rows of the crates, judging by how they stretched away for a good dozen yards. At the far end of the first row, he spotted the shadows. They were grouped tight, unmoving beneath the ceiling lights. And Bolan glimpsed the silhouetted muzzles of assault rifles.

Quiet and cautious, the soldier moved out. Beretta poised, he looked up at the catwalks. On the south walk he found nothing but darkened cubicles of offices. Likewise the east and west walks were vacant of roving sentries. Looking left, he discovered row after row of crates on pallets. One crate was left out, midway down, against the north wall.

The warehouse looked mammoth. If there were guns in these countless crates, then there was enough hardware here to field armies of terrorists.

Watching the shadows, Bolan melted in between the crates. Swiftly he moved for the lone crate, staying beneath the edge of the catwalk, in case a sentry was directly above. He listened to the angry exchange from the deeper end of the warehouse. It was difficult to know how many numbers he was facing, but mentally he counted the voices and concentrated on what they were saying.

"Americans selling out their own! Who is to trust them!"

"Our leader in the jihad believes they can be trusted. Up to a point."

"Abu sent three of our own tonight to Long Island."

"Are you saying his devotion and loyalty are questionable?"

"Hamil, I believe Abdul is merely saying we should be more careful of these American devils. Must I remind you, they have attacked us in our part of the world. Remember what just happened recently in Lebanon?"

"They killed our rivals."

"Tomorrow we will strike a blow for the jihad."

Bolan crouched beside the crate. The next day some monstrous act of terrorism was going to strike the city. Worse, it sounded as if Rawlins was right. Americans had sold out their own. But why? Money? Vengeance? Warped ideology?

"We are all prepared to sacrifice our lives, my brothers, to carry the single greatest day of vengeance our people have ever known!"

"Do you say we must be grateful to the Americans, these soldiers who betrayed their own people?"

Six men, Bolan figured, and there could be more in the building somewhere, even outside.

Their arguing became even more heated.

"We have been paid well by the American devils."

"Abu feeds us only dog scraps. He holds back our money."

"This is not only about money. Do not be fools. Praising money like the American devils."

With his commando dagger, Bolan pried the lid off the crate. Sliding the lid back a few inches, he found a dozen AK-47s. There was no marking on the crate to indicate its origin, nor was there any labeling to even disguise what was inside. Looking around at the crates, he couldn't even begin to count them all. But whatever the contents, the soldier couldn't let the crates reach their final destination.

Suddenly a shadow loomed over Bolan.

"It is not a question of gratitude, Jamal! We have pledged to fight to the death—"

"How can I sleep when all of you are squawking like old women!"

Bolan was looking up just as the bearded face stared down.

The Beretta was up and tracking as the man shouted, "Intruder!"

Just as the Arab gunman brought his AK-47 to bear on Bolan, the Beretta sneezed once, the 9 mm slug coring a neat red hole in the guard's forehead. Wild autofire spit from the gunman's assault rifle, spraying lead across the warehouse. Death throes sent the gunman spinning through the flimsy wood railing.

Chaos erupted from beyond Bolan's position. Cursing and yelling, bolts cocking on assault rifles, the guards propelled Bolan into the only course of action left.

Holstering the Beretta, he unslung the M-16.

As he darted down an aisle, a din of autofire struck the concrete in his wake, tracking on in a finger of spraying stone fragments.

Bolan escaped one instant of danger only to find the enemy had moved and gained a sudden advantage that could end it before it even began.

The soldier caught a glimpse of three angry faces before they cut loose from the west catwalk with a barrage of AK autofire.

A rain of hot lead descended near Bolan's position and swept toward him.

6

On the fly, Bolan felt wood chips eating at the back of his neck while tracking lead burned the air behind him. Lightning reflexes saved him, but only for the moment, as he leaped behind a stack of crates. Streams of autofire gouged wood and whined off concrete.

Too close for comfort, and he knew he had to make an instant life-or-death decision.

It was made. Risky, no doubt, knowing he had to expose himself to do what was necessary to strike back and rip the heart out of the high-ground gunners.

Moving low behind the crates, he gave his immediate surroundings a quick search. So far, nothing behind, nothing ahead. One long aisle was to his left flank, with crates stacked haphazardly in threes or fours. Gaining the high ground was critical, but he'd lost that edge.

Mentally he gauged the position from which the trio on the catwalk fired their weapons. They had moved as fast as a serpent strikes, taken the advantage he would have wanted. Clearly they had already made some contingency plan in the event they were raided—take the high ground and fight. These men weren't fanatic rabble; they seemed disciplined to some degree. Either they had military background or were trained by someone with military and combat experience.

If that was true, the ground force meant to outflank him. To stay put meant suicide.

Out of the corner of his eye, Bolan caught movement to his right. Whirling, catching the sounds of boots pounding concrete beyond his position, he triggered a short burst of 5.56 mm slugs. The savagely determined face of the enemy shrank from view as Bolan's autofire drove him to cover.

The soldier knew he was in danger of getting pinned.

Crouched, Bolan darted for another stack of crates. He triggered another burst as the rear gunman poked into view. Another miss.

"Where are they?"

"Keep moving!"

Low, Bolan scurried down a bisecting aisle, in a southerly direction. A break in the stacks exposed him long enough for the gunners on the catwalk to cut loose with another sustained burst of autofire. Scuttling on, ducking the new wave of bullets, Bolan made his decision.

It was now or never to turn the tide.

Still on the run, he popped up and sighted the trio of hardmen on the catwalk. Bolan triggered the M-203 as wood fragments flayed the side of his face. Streaking at 74.5 meters per second, the grenade took barely long enough for the gunmen up there to scream in terror, try to outrun the missile.

Not good enough.

The thunderous explosion rocked the building. Shouts of outrage abruptly ceased as torn-scarecrow figures went airborne on the ball of fire.

Spinning, aware potential death still dogged him from behind, Bolan triggered the M-16 at the gunman on his tail. The Arab bolted for cover, barely escaping the blaze of 5.56 mm lead. Bolan ceased fire, waited a split second, then saw the face whip back into sight. Bullets from the M-16 chewed wood for several heartbeats before factor number two added fuel to his fire.

A burst of autofire chattered from the direction of the hardman on his rear. A brief cry of pain, then the lone gunman from that direction danced into Bolan's view, blood spurting from the terrorist's chest. In one final act of desperation, the hardman held back on the trigger of his assault rifle, but a follow-up burst of gunfire sent him toppling to the floor.

Rawlins.

Moving east, determined to meet the enemy head-on, Bolan caught a terrorist with a lightning burst to his chest as the gunman popped into his sights, toward the west end of the narrow aisle. The terrorist flew back, skidded on his side. Debris from the blast showered the crates around Bolan.

If possible, the Executioner wanted a live one.

He quickly swept the catwalks, finding them clear of gunmen. Then Bolan leaped onto the crate in front of him. It would be a hard climb, but he was seeking the high ground.

Combat senses on full alert, the soldier was bounding onto another crate when he glimpsed a gunman surge below him. The terrorist saw his fallen brother and was starting to turn when Bolan drilled a burst across his chest, barely beating the enemy to the draw. Screaming briefly in pain and outrage, the terrorist pitched to the ground, twitched, then lay still.

Wood groaned from above Bolan. Swinging up the M-16, he found a terrorist had the same idea about seizing the upper ground. The surprise on the terrorist's face became a bloody mask of agony as Bolan blew it off with a quick burst of lead.

Autofire stuttered from behind the Executioner. A man shouted in Arabic, then screamed in pain. It sounded to the Executioner as if Rawlins was working hard to keep pace.

Bolan bounded up the crates and took a moment's cover. Eyes scanning his flanks, rear and the catwalks, the Executioner pulled a 30-round magazine from his satchel. He dropped the spent clip and rammed the fresh mag home.

There was a sudden quiet, disturbed next only by the sound of boots pounding in the distance. He listened intently, then climbed up a crate. To the south it sounded like two pairs of boots.

Bolan secured the high ground, four crates up off the floor, his flanks protected from weapons fire by crates piled higher to either side. Below he spotted two gunmen fleeing for an exit door. One was furiously punching in the numbers on a cellular phone. The other gunman was fanning the warehouse with fire from his AK-47, his wild eyes searching for a target.

Bolan didn't give him a chance to verify an invader. Flipping the selector switch for single shot, the Executioner went for a hostage. A sizzling 5.56 mm round tore high into the chest of Wild Eyes, who screamed in pain, his assault rifle flying away before he was hammered to the floor.

The gunner with the cellular phone wheeled, his mouth wide in outrage and fear at the sight of another lightning strike. Whether he was calling in reinforcements or alerting the safehouse they were under attack, it didn't matter to Bolan. One live one was all the soldier needed.

Another squeeze of the trigger, and the Executioner pumped off an expert killing shot. Downrange the cellular phone exploded into useless fragments before the slug shattered the skull and put the terrorist's lights out for good.

Bounding off the crates, the Executioner hit the floor and found the warehouse proper empty. Then a figure appeared from around the far west aisle. Bolan checked his fire as Rawlins stepped into view.

Striding on, Bolan loomed over the wounded terrorist. Hate blazed through the pain in the dark eyes staring up at the warrior. The terrorist's chest was soaked in blood, but the slug appeared to have passed clean through, just below the collarbone.

Bolan aimed the M-16 at the terrorist's face. "How many others are here?"

The man hesitated. Adjusting his aim, Bolan sent a round screaming off the concrete beside the terrorist's head.

"Nine!"

Bolan glanced at Rawlins who said, "I nailed two."

It added up. Turning grim attention back to his captive, Bolan said, "You're the last. I'm going to ask some questions. If I don't like what I hear, if I believe you're even thinking about lying to me, I'll shoot you. Nod if you understand."

The Arab nodded, cursing Bolan.

"Sounds like you want to live. Are all these crates filled with weapons?"

"Yes. Enough to kill thousands of infidels!"

"Tomorrow you've planned an attack?"

"Yes."

"When and where?"

The terrorist clenched his teeth in defiance. Bolan put the muzzle against his forehead.

The Arab squirmed as fear bulged his eyes. ''Hamil, he knew the details. We weren't to be told anything until the morning. I swear! That's the truth!''

''Do you have explosives in these crates?''

''Yes. Plastique and dynamite.''

''Where?''

The terrorist looked toward Rawlins. ''Down there. Last stack.''

''Open those crates and check it,'' Bolan told the agent. Bolan thought ahead. Somehow he needed to get to Abu. Now he had a trump card. The prisoner would be his messenger, and the soldier was going to leave a message here before he left.

''Your safehouse in the Bronx. How many are there?''

''Four,'' he spit.

''Another cache of weapons? Is Abu there?''

The terrorist looked away, and Bolan knew he wanted to hide something. Another whine of lead striking the concrete made him jump, instantly reassess his decision to lie.

''Abbas may or may not be there, I cannot say for certain. The only weapons there are the ones my brothers carry to protect themselves against infidels.''

''Are you protecting something at this safehouse? Answer me quickly.''

''Money. Our pay for our mission.''

''How much?'' Bolan asked.

''Two million. U.S. dollars.''

''Do you know who owns this warehouse?''

''Germans. They deliver the guns and the explosives.''

''Do you know a man named Max Tielig?''

Confusion showed in the terrorist's eyes. He shook his head, groaned in pain. "Germans, I don't know their names. Well dressed. They have money, they're arrogant pigs. Treat us like mere camel dung…"

"Skip the self-pity. All these weapons, some of them were going someplace in particular. Was there a buyer? Your immediate future depends on what you tell me."

"I know a man from New Jersey came here yesterday. Big American. Sternmann, that was his name. He met with us. It was arranged already he would get a shipment from the Germans. It left earlier today. I know Sternmann owns some security company, I heard…Stick or Sticks Security. He made a joke about some river."

Bolan paused. Hydra. Now Styx. Mere coincidence? Or something else? Whatever, the soldier was compiling a shopping list of targets to visit. First the warehouse. Then the safehouse. It would be a double blow to Abu's operation. Level the warehouse, seize the money. Whoever who was sponsoring Abu would likewise get the hard message.

"There was an attack out in Long Island tonight. A former senator named O'Malley was killed," Bolan said. "Who planned it and why? Don't lie to me—I overheard you talking about it."

"An American soldier, formerly of your Special Forces."

"Ben Calhoun?"

The terrorist nodded. "He hired us. He trained us."

The picture was becoming more sordid, but at least the soldier was getting confirmation of the enemy. He heard Rawlins whistle. "What?" Bolan said as Rawlins walked toward him.

"There must be three, four hundred pounds of explosives, between the dynamite and the C-4. Could be more.

Time delays for the most part, looks they wanted to make it easy on themselves. Set the timer and run like hell. A kid could do it.''

"I'll take a look."

"I've also got detonating cord, radio remote and primer cord for the C-4," Rawlins said. "These guys were serious about whatever it is they were going to do."

"Are doing," Bolan told the agent, then pinned the terrorist with a steely gaze. "You're going to leave with us. I want you to go to Abu. Tell him he's on his way out of business." Bolan asked Rawlins if he had another safehouse they could use other than the one he had on the Lower East Side.

"Affirmative. Why?"

Bolan gave the terrorist the address and location of Rawlins's safehouse in the bad part of town. "Can you remember that?"

"Believe me, infidel, I will tell him. And he will find you."

"I'm counting on that."

Bolan stood and turned to Rawlins. "Watch him. He'll leave with us."

"Are you going to do what I think you're going to do, Belasko?"

"And then some."

The Executioner started to get busy. He was shaking the trees hard, and the snakes, he knew, were only beginning to fall.

COUNTDOWN TO ABU'S doomsday message was ticking rapidly as Rawlins headed them west on the Cross-Bronx Expressway. Bolan watched the numbers roll down on his chronometer. Ten, nine, eight...

Back at the warehouse, he had placed fifty pounds of

dynamite and a comparable charge of C-4 around the warehouse. He had set the timers to let them clear the scene. What was about to happen would tie up this borough for the rest of the night and well into the next day, breathing room to let them proceed to the next step.

Abu's potential killing factory was history, about to be an angry memory for the Palestinian who nicknamed himself Hannibal. And whoever fronted the warehouse for terrorists would be found out and paid an unwelcome visit by Bolan.

Before leaving, the soldier had confiscated forty pounds of C-4, with primer and radio remote boxes. It might come in handy, and it was too good an opportunity to pass up. The spoils of war seemed to be adding up, and best of all, Abu would get the message within the hour from the terrorist Bolan had left alive. Somehow the soldier had to reel Abu in. From there, he believed he could get to Calhoun. The ex-major, the soldier knew, held the key to critical answers.

The countdown hit zero, and the fireworks began.

A half mile from ground zero, Bolan heard the hellish roar that split the night asunder. In his side mirror, he watched as the giant fireball mushroomed, turned the Bronx night into day, uprooting the warehouse, pulping it from the inside out. Anything inside that inferno, man or metal, was vaporized.

Rawlins whistled at the sight of the fireball. "You don't pull any punches, do you, cowboy?"

"All I need to know from you is if you're with me. No matter what."

Rawlins turned and looked Bolan square in the eye. "I know something about dirty tactics, Belasko. Whatever you've got in mind, I don't see where I've got any choice but to ride with the program."

"I thought you told me there's always a choice."

"You've gotten results, Belasko. I ride. Let's just hope this isn't a one-way ride."

The glow from the monstrous blast was so strong, Bolan clearly saw the hard frown etched on the agent's face.

HIDDEN PERSONAL agendas seemed to be bonding together the unlikeliest of allies. Former U.S. military men had joined forces with Palestinian terrorists who had been infiltrated into New York for some horrific scheme.

So far, Bolan had no clue—other than money, warped pride and ultimate power—as to what might be driving an enemy he was slowly but surely flushing out of the dark. He wondered if it was as simple as basic greed and ambition, or was he faced with a threat he had never before dealt with?

Either way, the soldier was blitzing on, fast and furious.

Starting now.

Next was a one-story frame house, near the Harlem River. Through the shadows of the front yard, Bolan made the door. Even at that predawn hour, light still shone on the curtain of the living-room window. Inside the targets were still awake, hungry for the morning and whatever their insidious plan might be. If Abu was there, it would be sweet icing.

Bolan's plan for this hit had been made on the drive to this target.

Bolan checked his chronometer. The rental car was parked down the alley that butted up against the house. Rawlins had already moved in, a custom-made sound suppressor attached to his Glock.

The man should be in position at the back door, Bolan

knew. It was the money the Executioner was after. Rubbing more salt into Abu's wounds should bring the man howling for vengeance.

Bolan imagined he could almost hear Rawlins rap on the back door. In fact he was sure of it as he saw a shadow roll against the curtain, disappear to check who was at the back door at that hour.

With the silenced Beretta poised to fire, the Executioner gave the residential street one last look. Nothing.

The soldier raised his foot and kicked in the front door. He went in low, and from the doorway off to his side, he saw two hardmen wheel his way, armed with AK-47s. In that instant he also heard a familiar chugging sound, followed by the loud thud of a body. Rawlins was making his play.

Bolan had his prey dead to rights and wasn't about to lose the edge. One terrorist was greeted by a 9 mm slug, just as he finished his spin to lay eyes on the big American's hardware. Bone cracked under the slug's impact, and the gunner dropped in the wide doorway. Bolan saw the other gunman hesitate as blood from his fallen comrade smeared his face and shock hardened his features.

"Toss your weapon away from you!" Bolan growled. "On your knees and hands behind your head! Do it!"

As the weapon clunked to the living-room floor, Bolan sighted a figure rushing out of a door to his side. A chatter of autofire burned the air, but the soldier was already diving behind the couch. Cotton stuffing blew overhead, and bullets thudded into yielding cushion.

Sliding to the end of the couch, the Executioner popped up, aware the brief leadstorm was still slamming his former position. A single slug from the Beretta cored the gunman's skull, as the soldier got to his feet.

The terrorist was still on his knees, fingers laced behind his head. Another of Abu's cronies wanted life over certain death.

"Belasko, it's me. I'm coming through. I'm clear out here."

Rawlins came through what Bolan assumed was the kitchen doorway.

"Check the house," Bolan told Rawlins.

"You," he said to the terrorist. "I know about the money. Where is it?" Defiance stared back at Bolan. "Whether you're dead or alive, I'll find it."

A second later Rawlins approached Bolan. "We're clear, but we need to get moving."

"The money?"

"You will pay for this, infidel."

"Wrong. You're paying for it." Bolan walked up to the terrorist and rested the muzzle between his eyes. "Last chance."

The Arab paused, swallowed hard, then growled, "Bedroom closet. Brown suitcase."

Bolan pulled the Beretta back as Rawlins moved. Moments later the agent's penchant for whistling signaled Bolan they had struck paydirt.

The Executioner told the terrorist, "I've got a message for you to deliver to your boss."

7

The mere sight of the two Palestinians disgusted Calhoun. His blood still boiling from what they had told him, the ex–Special Forces major fell in step behind the Arabs as three of his own men led the way down the treacherous stairway.

The one called Abdul was bleeding, and the other Arab, Jabaz, looked ready to faint from fear. Blood and terror, Calhoun knew, would soon be the least and the last of their problems. Failure could be rewarded only one way.

Against his explicit orders, Abu began to question his comrades about the two hits. If it was true—the warehouse and its massive stockpile of Russian hardware gone up in flames, plus the Bronx safehouse hit by an unknown opposition—Calhoun smelled trouble ahead. He needed answers quickly. He had come too far, worked too hard to fall back in defeat of any kind.

"Shut up," Calhoun snarled into Abu's ear. "I'll do the talking."

With sound suppressors attached to their Ingram M-10s, Calhoun watched as Augustly, Morrow and Billerton hit the bottom of the steps and fanned out. It was an abandoned building of some type near the East River on the Queens side. Only an hour ago, Abu had gotten the SOS from his comrades. One call of distress had followed the other. The pickup had been arranged as soon as Calhoun heard the news.

Now it was just after dawn, and the hubbub of New York began outside.

"Sweep and secure," Calhoun ordered his three soldiers. He indicated that the Palestinians should move to the far wall. Large black rats skittered across the floor, and shadows flitted down a narrow corridor that reeked of urine and vomit. Moments later the rats were scattering pell-mell as Calhoun saw his men unleash their weapons on whoever had the misfortune of making the place home for the night. There was a short scream, and another shadow bolted from between slabs of rubble. But Augustly's shaved bullet head shone in a glow of firelight from one of the rooms down there, and he dropped the runner with a bloody line of bullet holes up the spine. Three muzzles then chugged out long streams into each room. Someone pleaded for mercy but found only eternity.

Calhoun waited, then the lean, blond Morrow informed him, "We're clear, Major. Just a few crack addicts and winos."

Under different circumstances, Calhoun would have smiled. Junkies were among the many undesirables on a long list of human disease that Calhoun knew the world would soon be cured of. That they fed the disease with narcotics and black-market weapons to street gangs across the country was simply a means to an end. Feeding the criminal element in America was merely a stepping-stone to building the Coalition's vision of a better tomorrow. Someday soon the world was going to be a better place.

"How could you let this happen!" Abu raged at his comrades in the jihad. "I have lost two million dollars."

The cellular phone rang inside Calhoun's overcoat. He pulled it from a pocket and punched it on. It was his man on-site in the Bronx.

Calhoun listened to the bad news. "Yes. I see. I'll be in touch. Over." Cold fury in his eyes, Calhoun ran a look over the Palestinians before letting it settle on Abu. "And it looks like I've lost ten million. The warehouse was blown up halfway across the Bronx."

A trace of panic hit Abu's eyes. "Lucky for all of us you have other weapons depots in the city."

"Not luck, Abu. Good planning. You two, describe these two men who kicked your asses up around your teeth and sent you scurrying back to us like whipped dogs." He listened while they sputtered their report: big guy with cold eyes, moved as fast as a cheetah; the other one, tall, skinny with long salt-and-pepper hair, goatee. It should be easy enough to spot them if they were on his tail. From the sound of the report, Calhoun suspected the two hitters were professional killers. Any prisoners were taken as pawns for the next strike.

"Either one of you wonder why he let you live?"

Both Arabs flinched at the question as if it were a slap in the face. One shrugged as the other said, "He had a message...I was to give to Abbas."

"So you've given it. Abbas is going out of business. This unknown adversary says he'll give Abbas his money back but only if he turns me over. Somehow I get the feeling one or both of you ran off at the mouth about me. I bet he wanted to know if you knew me, and one or both of you confirmed it." They hesitated long enough for Calhoun to know they'd squawked about him. Again it was good planning that only Abu and a few of his cronies who were now en route for the heart of Manhattan knew the full details of what was going to happen.

"We could not tell him what we do not know!" the bleeder cried. "We did not even know how to find you!"

"He asked about what happened on Long Island, who and what was behind it," the whiner said. "He knew about it somehow. About the senator."

"How stupid you two are!" Calhoun rasped. "He knew because he was there. And did you stop and think for one moment while you were blubbering at his feet to save your miserable lives that he set you loose just so he could get to me?"

"They have given me an address in the Lower East Side where I can find them, Major," Abu said. "Let me go, I will take some men with me and—"

"It's a setup."

"Perhaps, Major. But I cannot just allow this person to take that kind of money from me and go unpunished. Nor," Abu continued, moderating his tone with a hint of respect, "would I think you would not want to see him dead after what he did to that shipment of arms."

Calhoun clenched his jaw, then rubbed his face. Problems were springing up out of nowhere. At least it was a good guess they weren't dealing with official law enforcement. No, it was cowboy action, hit and run. Calhoun had made plenty of enemies over the years, in many countries. Not to mention he was still doing business with the Colombians, who were as crazy as hell, and he never knew when they may turn on him.

"Let me go find these bastards and bring back their heads!"

Calhoun looked at Abu. "No. I can't afford to have you out of my sight. In a few short hours, I need you to brief your men and help coordinate the attacks from our command center.''

''But—''

Calhoun cut off Abu's interruption in the next instant. Whipping the MAC-10 from beneath his overcoat, Calhoun squeezed off two short bursts of 9 mm death, marching bloody holes across the chests of the two men. They crumpled into boneless sprawls at Abu's feet.

Rage and disbelief hardened Abu's eyes.

''However,'' Calhoun said, ''I will assign three of your men to go to this address and try their luck. If they don't succeed, they had better get the first plane to the Middle East. Do you understand me, Abu? Do you understand the importance of what we, you, are going to do today in this country you despise so much?''

''I do.''

''Convince me, then.'' He nodded at the dead Arabs. ''I'll make that up to you. Succeed, I'll see you get satisfactory compensation. I hope you're not overly upset about those two.''

Abu glowered at the dead men. ''In your place I would have done the same thing.''

Calhoun nodded. ''Good enough.''

When Abu had been recruited by Calhoun's own sponsors, he had figured, from what he knew of the Palestinian back then, that the terrorist was driven more by greed than ideology. Unless greed was tempered by principles and clearly defined goals, Calhoun knew greedy men got careless. Abu was proving himself a liability. After the New York operation, he wouldn't need the Palestinian anymore.

''We proceed on schedule,'' he concluded, then ordered Morrow and Billerton to escort Abu to their vehicle.

When they were alone, Augustly moved up behind Calhoun. The giant fanned the gloom with a wary gaze, as if not trusting they were alone.

"What do you think, Major?"

"Problems, that's what I think. You say Tielig's been shadowed the past two days?"

"They had Company written all over them."

"Find them. Take care of them, then report back to base."

"Whoever hit the warehouse and the Arabs is playing hardball, Major. You think we're up against a black-ops team that has found us out?"

"Before show time I intend to find out. When I do, they'll know they've grabbed the bull by the horns. Keep your eyes peeled."

Calhoun made the first call. After eight rings he heard the gruff German voice on the other end. "Sorry to wake you, Max. We need a face-to-face this morning. I'll send a man right away."

"I hear trouble in your voice," the German businessman growled.

"No trouble. But I suggest you get your bags packed and make flight arrangements."

"Why? What are you talking about?"

"Unless you want to get hung up in New York for a few more days, you might want to be ready to fly out by twelve, no later than 1300. I'll explain when I see you."

The German was grumbling he didn't understand, but Calhoun cut him off and made the next call. When the man came on, Calhoun said, "There may be a problem. The warehouse was hit."

He heard Sternmann say, "Really. That's not good. Our people never made it back. Not a word."

"I know that. Your guess is as good as mine what happened to them."

"Law problems?"

"Someone's hitting the operation, but they seem to be nipping away at the fringes. How much they know and who they are, I can't say at the moment. I'll need the rest of the money for the shipment ASAP."

"I'm working on it. My buyer's only sent half payment so far. The truck's still sitting here, but I may move it in light of these new developments. I have some options."

"I don't. You'll get a fax from me this morning. Will it be a problem for you to meet with me?"

"You mean to deliver payment personally?"

"It isn't that I don't trust you, but we may need to cover some items for the future."

"I'll be here."

Calhoun hung up. Sternmann was another loose end, a liability that could lead trouble his way, he thought. Calhoun didn't need the kind of problems he was suddenly faced with shadowing him out-of-country. Their relationship had served its purpose.

It was time to call the Colombians.

WATCHING THE TENEMENT building from an alley across the street, Bolan listened to the last of Brognola's report. Moments ago the soldier had finished tallying the previous night's score for the big Fed.

"That's it from my end, Striker. If nothing else, Stony Man at least confirmed what Rawlins and O'Malley told you about the possibility of a renegade counterterrorist operation overseas."

"And the key players I want seem to have just disappeared after the attacks in Beirut, Jordan and Syria."

"Stands to reason that's how Calhoun met Abu."

"And recruited him. Something tells me someone is above Calhoun and wanted Abu to help field a terrorist army."

"Again, why have they resurfaced in New York? Plus now you've got this Sternmann, who owns Styx Security and Trucking in New Jersey. And we now know Muldare was former Special Forces and worked for Sternmann and was a member of Calhoun's Special Forces group in Nam. Almost all of Sternmann's employees either were or are ex-military. It appears Muldare did security work for a close friend of O'Malley's. Could have been Muldare came highly recommended to the late former senator. I wish I had more for you."

"I've got a shopping list. It's good enough."

"We still have no clear answers or agenda on this, Striker. Kurtzman's working around the clock. It takes time to track the history on each potential player in this puzzle."

"I'll get answers somehow."

"As for the money trail, it may prove difficult to track. Bear did confirm McBain owns some cushy homes in the spots you've been told. Seems McBain made a few good investments on the stock market. But from what we can tell on this end, not good enough to cover the overhead he's acquired on three different properties."

"So other than globe-trotting and spending money, no one can tell what McBain's really been doing?"

"Sounds like it falls back to what's happening up there."

"One last thing. I'll need our ace pilot on standby," Bolan said, referring to his friend and top gun, Jack Grimaldi. Brognola confirmed he would do that, make any necessary preparations for landing sites at a moment's notice. Brognola wished Bolan luck and told him to watch his back before they severed the connection.

A ghost of a smile traced Rawlins's lips as he glanced at Bolan. "Your boss confirm a lot of what I told you?"

For the time being, Bolan decided it was best not to ask the man any questions or antagonize him.

Silently they watched and waited. It was just after sunrise, and cars were slowly rolling down the street, with signs of humanity scuttling from the buildings. If Abu had gotten the message, Bolan should know soon enough. An open firefight on the street with innocents who could get caught in the crossfire was the last thing Bolan wanted. He was looking for some advantage of surprise, overtake them without the enemy getting off the first shot. Of course, Abu—if and when he showed— would be on high alert. Anything could happen.

A few minutes later, a dark sedan slid in front of the building. Two long-haired, bearded men in overcoats exited from the vehicle. There were noticeable bulges beneath their coats. The driver had double-parked and kept the engine running.

"You take the driver, but I want him alive. Wait for me," Bolan directed.

As luck would have it, the driver rolled down the window and fired up a cigarette. He watched his comrades disappear through the tenement's doorway. He should have been watching his back because Rawlins made his move, sweeping up on the driver and sticking the muzzle of his Glock in the man's ear.

"Slide over and don't move," Bolan heard the agent order.

After a quick check of the street and sidewalk to see if they were being watched, Bolan entered the building.

The hallway was as grim and lifeless as he'd first found it. Other than a baby crying from somewhere in the building, it was silent.

The Executioner drew his silenced Beretta. He saw the door to Rawlins's apartment already opened, but knew the hitters had a half-minute head start.

A few seconds later, they emerged from the apartment, still wielding silenced mini-Uzis. If he couldn't get answers, the soldier could shave the odds. The fewer enemy numbers biting at his heels, the better.

At first the Arab gunmen looked disappointed from not having found someone inside to kill. When they saw Bolan take a step toward them from the shadows, fear and surprise lit their faces.

With a one-two punch, the Beretta whispering in his fist, Bolan doused their lights with one 9 mm slug each between the eyes. As they crumpled to the hall floor, Bolan was already moving through the door.

Piling into the back of the sedan, Bolan asked the driver, "Can you reach Abu?" Silence. "Your life depends on your cooperation."

"Yes. I am to call him right away."

"Make the call. We'll park this in the alley and take my vehicle," Bolan told Rawlins.

Using the cellular phone he had brought with him, the Arab called, tension etched on his features. Bolan waited. The man started to speak angry words in Arabic, but Bolan nudged him in the back of the head with his Beretta and growled, "English."

"He wants to know if you have his money," the Arab said.

"Tell him we meet first. We'll talk about it."

The Arab relayed the message, then said, "He'll meet you in Central Park."

"It's a big park," Bolan said.

"Central Park South. He'll have a man waiting for us at the Grand Army Plaza."

Bolan made eye contact with Rawlins. Both of them knew their prisoner could be marching them into a trap.

Again, though, the soldier saw no choice but to play out whatever hand was being dealt.

"You want me to call my people as backup, Belasko?"

Bolan didn't want any more unknown allies by his side. "No."

8

To his surprise Calhoun found Max Tielig taking the news about the sudden rash of trouble better than expected. A few grunts from the German, a couple of nods, but no outbursts of anger or indignation. After Calhoun's initial report about the loss of Tielig's merchandise in the previous night's attack, they strolled away from the pond in Central Park.

While the silence lingered between them, Calhoun checked his surroundings, alert for anything that looked out of the ordinary. The brisk but sunny morning had brought out small armies of cyclists, joggers, boaters, skateboarders and bird-watchers. All looked normal. No furtive shadows danced around the oaks and maples, no suits with radio receivers in their ears. While jaded New Yorkers frolicked in this green carpet stretched at the foot of the surrounding Manhattan skyline, Calhoun was there to cement some final and deadly serious business, affairs reaching overseas, he knew, that would breathe new life into the Coalition.

Dressed in an expensive topcoat, Tielig stared down in the water, which mirrored the Manhattan skyline, as they walked over a bridge. Behind, Tielig's security force of three grim-faced men in dark shades monitored the rear. Ahead, somewhere on his side of East Drive, Calhoun knew the Colombians waited. On short notice, he had brought together two groups of his key players. At the moment all he could deliver was bad omens and promises of final payment.

The short, stocky, bullnecked German smoothed back his immaculately coiffed white hair. "Have you forgotten who supplies me, Major? Thus supplies you and your wholesalers. When trouble starts for men such as us, it all has a domino effect."

"I'm fully aware, Max, who I have to answer. Russians. Specifically the Russian Mafia, which is linked with another group you don't even want to know about. And it was me who introduced them to you to help you bail out of several bad business deals you blundered into."

Tielig winced at either the mention of brutal men he would rather not be involved with, or his own recent personal failures. Calhoun didn't care about the man's distress. But Calhoun's sponsors needed the German's shell companies to funnel their own illicit funds, needed his ships that traveled established routes around the world to transport their own merchandise and needed his shady connections in the Far East.

"I'm glad you asked me here," the German said, clasping his hands behind his back. "The park this time of morning, it is especially beautiful. Truly a man-made marvel, ingenious—840 acres. Were you aware there are two hundred species of birds—?"

"Max, I'm short on time. First order of business, I want you to know you had a problem that found you out."

"Which was?"

"The CIA. They've been following you for two days that my men know of. Don't worry, they were taken care of about an hour ago."

Tielig scowled. "How do you know they were CIA? Why would they suspect anything of me?"

"You want details about getting information out of men?"

Tielig shook his head. "I am sure your methods produce results. Be that as it may, you bring me trouble I don't need."

"I consider it a challenge, Max, not trouble."

"Whatever. See things from my side of it. My warehouse is destroyed, merchandise for which I have not been fully paid—"

"You'll get the rest of your money."

"Forgive me if I seem skeptical. Second you have an agenda of your own. Third you surround yourself with a known international criminal." He looked over his shoulder to where Abu, flanked by Billerton and Augustly, was walking behind Tielig's security trio. "You do business with the Colombians, whom I have never cared for, by the way, using my ships as transport for their merchandise. Somehow you don't strike me as a narcotics trafficker."

The German was whining. Calhoun fought down a rising irritation to grab him by the lapel and slap some truth into him. Where Tielig referred to merchandise as goods bartered for money, Calhoun felt grateful that at least Abu understood merchandise in terms of human flesh turned warrior. Calhoun brought himself down to Tielig's bottom-line dollar level.

"You've been paid, Max."

"But I have suffered a most annoying setback. Fortunately my tracks are covered as far as my affairs in this country go. However, if word gets out of this fiasco with the warehouse, I could take, as you Americans would say, a bath in this endeavor. Not to mention my entire life would be put under close and intense scrutiny by the authorities.''

Calhoun clenched his jaw. ''It isn't about money, Max.''

''Then what?''

Calhoun felt a fire stir in his belly. Too many memories to pick through boiled into mind. In a flash of anger, though, it all came together and made the ultimate destination within reach, not to mention the one and only truth.

''It's about how this country has sold out, a nation I put my life on the line for but was myself sold out and by my own. A country that was once great and righteous, which I used to believe in, but came to see a profound light, and how its selling out is merely dragging the rest of the world toward the edge of the abyss. It's about how our government does business with criminals and thugs and dictators, and parades it under the noses of a public it considers the ignorant, the unwashed and the unworthy. It's how this government and its intelligence agencies—and I know this for a fact—have engineered and created and now support the largest and wealthiest criminal enterprises the world has ever known. They espouse virtue and cry for human rights while they look the other way at genocide that is happening in countries rarely mentioned, and even as we speak.

''They say on the one hand they hold hands with the devil to keep world peace, maintain the status quo. While on the other hand they're fattening their pockets and pulling up the drawbridge because they know the world situation is out of control with no hope in sight— only a huge mushroom cloud on the horizon to keep the starving hordes from taking what they have. It's containment, Max, or conquer and divide. I and the people who sponsor me are about eliminating corruption and chaos in the world by shoving it all back in their face and restoring humanity to human beings.''

"By spreading more corruption and chaos?"

"By showing them we can do it better. By making generous offers no sane man would refuse once he sees what's in it for him. In time the smart and the sane will be brought under our umbrella.''

"You mean your umbrella. And these sponsors."

Calhoun put some edge in his voice. "Max, my sponsors are many, and they are very powerful men, far more powerful, with far more money and clout than you can dream of.''

"But you need my legitimacy as a cover to help further your agenda.''

"I need to prove I can get the job done. Starting today.''

"Referring in your mysterious way, I gather, to something that is about to happen in this city.''

"I would heed my advice, Max. I'm playing for keeps. Whoever and whatever gets in my way is going down. I've got everything to live for, Max, because, hey, I've got a dream. But I also don't give a damn about dying because I've already helped to do what must be done. I have set something in motion that will change the face of mankind forever.''

"Major, I don't pretend to understand you or your motives. As for your sponsors, my own intelligence sources warn me they are a sordid group of individuals I would do best to put great distance to. What I know is that, yes, I have been paid handsomely by an associate of yours. Money rolls in—I see no evil, hear no evil. With me there is nothing else to consider but the bottom line—money. I am a businessman, not a mercenary.''

"And our business isn't concluded, Max."

"You needn't remind, Major. I am sure you will contact me shortly about moving merchandise we have discussed to the east. I have not done business in Pakistan before, you understand—"

"But you'll see to the details, I assume."

"And I assume when I return home, you will send a man with the necessary funds?"

"You can count on me, Max. Question is, can I count on you?"

Tielig scowled. "I will deliver. On that cordial promise, you'll excuse me."

"Have a nice flight home, Max."

He was watching Tielig and his security force departing when Calhoun spotted Abu on his cellular. The man barked in Arabic, at first, then lowered his voice, turning away as Calhoun stared at him. Judging Abu's violent reaction, Calhoun knew the Arabs he'd handpicked had been marched to their deaths. Not only had he expected as much, but he also wanted it that way. If it played out as previously, there would be a messenger. Only now, the unknown enemy would come attached to the errand boy. A showdown with the faceless enemy on his heels was necessary.

Ordering Abu brought to him, Calhoun strode on down a trail. Ahead, he saw Eduardo Santiago. Sitting on a bench in a clearing, the Colombian diplomat was feeding pigeons. The dark-haired, lean, mustachioed Santiago had his four-man security force nearby. Beneath their overcoats, Calhoun saw the bulges of large handguns, perhaps even compact machine guns.

As he walked toward the diplomat, it struck Calhoun just how deep and intricate the Coalition had woven the web of its operation. Like many others in positions of power, Santiago was bought and paid for. First by Calhoun's sponsors, who could come as deadly shadow men in the middle of night with an offer of either great wealth or certain death. Second a growing offshoot of the Cali cartel had enlisted Santiago as its own personal middleman to establish new drug pipelines. Often Santiago would bring in shipments aboard his jet under the guise of international cooperation on the war on drugs.

Calhoun glanced at Abu. "More bad news?"

"They are coming here."

"Your desire to get your money back exceeds your common sense. I take it they want to exchange the money for my head."

"We can kill them right here."

Calhoun had already determined he would. Since the news of the previous night's hits, he knew it was all going to the wall. He had been smelled out and now he was being hunted. Even still, staging an encounter with the enemy in public risked throwing away the whole operation if he was killed or captured, which wasn't an option.

So, they would have their face-to-face with these unknown attackers. An all-out hit-and-run firefight in the park may prove the only way to eliminate the threat. Having briefed his people on a potential engagement in the park, he ordered Billerton to get two three-man teams in position. Then he told Abu to go rendezvous with the enemy where they had agreed. Searching the grassy knolls and the latticework of trees and shrubbery on either side of the trail, Calhoun trusted his snipers to find concealment.

"I'll send two of my own men with you, Abu."

"I am beginning to think you knew this was all going to happen just this way. I am starting to believe we have been nothing but pawns in some game you are playing. I wonder if I should even continue to play this game of yours and have nothing in the end, not even my money, to show for the blood and the sacrifice of what is happening."

Augustly patched the order through for an escort.

Calhoun dismissed the Arab's resentment. "I'll wait here. You and me, we'll settle up later."

Morrow arrived and led the Arab away. Ignoring Abu's angry gaze, Calhoun told his man, "'We're walking out of here.' Pass that code on to our sniper teams. Once I get a fix on this situation, I want it resolved. Quick and clean. This thing's going to turn messy. If Abu gets cute, I want him taken out. I'll deal with the operation personally from here on."

"Aye, aye, Major."

Calhoun strode for Santiago as several teenage in-line skaters swept by. There were plenty of human shields, in case it went bad.

"Señor Calhoun, I believe we have much to discuss." The Colombian didn't bother to look up as he threw a handful of bread crumbs to the scavengers. "Señor Maldonado is unhappy the rest of the funds are being held up."

"I can explain."

"Please do." The Colombian looked over as Calhoun took a seat beside him. "You understand the shipment is ready to go. The vessel you sent from the Germans is docked. If it sits where it is, it could draw unwanted attention."

"I need another day, two at the outside."

"That may prove unacceptable."

"Then I need a face-to-face with Maldonado."

Calhoun smiled as he read the Colombian's concern.

"You ask for a lot, Major."

"I'm delivering a lot. Just pass the word on. Or do you want me to just show up unannounced? Force my hand, and I'll piss on somebody's parade."

With another glance around the trail and the rolling, tree-studded landscape, the more Calhoun believed it was the perfect killzone. This smug and dirty little errand boy for the cartel may have to take a stray bullet. Another loose end, more mystery and confusion thrown in his wake. Oh, well. With or without the diplomat, his shipment was guaranteed.

In short order Calhoun would tend to Maldonado and his Cali thugs personally. They weren't aware of it yet, but even the Cali cartel was about to play ball with the Coalition. Or they would all suffer slow and agonizing death.

It was high time, Calhoun thought, to start taking care of business his way. And it was going to begin with his unknown opposition in the park.

ARMED TO TAKE ON whatever enemy numbers showed, Bolan was entering Central Park, angling for the pond, when he spotted Abu. Beneath his overcoat, Bolan had the Uzi on a swivel rig. In his pockets he carried two frag grenades. Rawlins had parked the rental in a nearby garage. The agent was ordered to fall back, shadow Bolan's rear. Before abandoning the Arab's vehicle, the soldier had checked the trunk, found a compact MAC-10 and spare clips. Rawlins was now blessed with another gift from the enemy.

Both men knew the meet could fall south in a hurry. But Bolan was counting on a lethal engagement. At that point he needed concrete answers to whatever the terrorists had designed to unleash on the city.

Unfortunately innocents were out in force. In a way an all-out roving firefight was unacceptable to Bolan. First he didn't want the blood of civilians on his hands. Second he couldn't afford to get cornered by NYPD.

Again the soldier's options were limited to what the enemy dictated.

Two Americans trailed Abu, weapons clearly outlined beneath their overcoats. Bolan kept his prisoner in front of him, the Desert Eagle in his fist, buried in a large side pocket.

"Abbas," the hostage cried. "There was nothing we could do."

"Silence, Afil! You!" Abu snarled at Bolan. "So, you are the one who is causing us all so much trouble."

"You know what I want," Bolan said. "Let's get on with this."

"Where is my money?"

"Where's Calhoun?"

Abu grinned wolfishly. "The major is anxious to meet with you."

"So let's not keep him waiting."

"You want the major, and I get my money, is that what you propose?"

"I'm prepared to offer alternatives."

Bolan watched the confusion shadow their faces.

The Executioner was told to follow. As he dropped in behind the enemy, he checked his flank. He gritted his teeth when he spotted Rawlins slip through a crowd of joggers in the distance. Bolan made brief eye contact with the agent. Three minutes was the standing order. Now Rawlins was nearly up his back.

If everyone seemed hell-bent on making his own rules for his own agenda, then the Executioner determined no

one there had yet to see how he could fling it all back
in their faces.

Whatever, the soldier knew the fuse was definitely lit,
and sizzling down fast.

Heading deeper into the park, the Executioner already knew the odds were stacked against him. When he finally arrived at the meet site, he found out right away just how formidable a task it would prove to even walk away breathing. His sudden appearance provoked an angry outburst by an unidentified player on the bench. Bolan gave his surroundings a sweeping overview but turned grim attention quickly on the unknown players ahead, his combat senses on full alert.

"What is the meaning of this? Who is this man?"

"This is a flea on the back of the tiger, Santiago."

"I am not here to play some game with you!" Santiago rasped. "I do not like surprises."

"This is no game, amigo. Relax and stay put," Calhoun warned the man, who glared for a long moment at Bolan, then lifted a restraining hand to his four bodyguards as they began to reach inside their coats. "So, you're the troubleshooter, huh?" Calhoun called out to Bolan. "What are you? CIA? DEA? Assassin from the Company's special-operations division?"

"None of the above. I'm a soldier, Calhoun. Like you once were."

"I still am a soldier, mister. Only now it's a different war."

Bolan told both Afil and Abu to stay close, not move, then said, "Where did it go wrong for you, Calhoun?"

"I got you, soldier." Calhoun laughed. "You're still living in a world where duty, honor and patriotism mean something. You see me as the bad guy. Have you been living in a glass bubble these past twenty years? It isn't me who went wrong. It's this country and the rest of the world that went wrong. I'm simply a soldier in a new war that's meant to make things right again. Now, if you're finished picking my brain, I'll make a suggestion that you turn around and just walk on. That's my one and only standing offer."

"I can't do that."

"Suit yourself. You're not big enough to stop what's already been set in motion."

"A man has to try."

Bunching up the back of his prisoner's coat, Bolan pulled Afil in tight. Another heated exchange briefly took place between Calhoun and Santiago. The dark-haired man tried to rise off the bench, but Calhoun shoved him down. Suddenly Calhoun drew his Ingram and thrust it at the Colombian.

Bolan tensed, ready for the situation to blow up in his face. A look of murderous intensity shone in Calhoun's eyes. Bolan surveyed his perimeter and sized up his chances.

The terrain on his left flank sloped away from the trail. A boulder here and there, trees and bushes. To his right some maple trees, then a small clearing, giving way to a gentle rise up a knoll that was lined with more trees and shrubbery. Up there, Bolan glimpsed gunmetal as at least three figures scuttled into view. Snipers. They fanned out and positioned themselves behind trees. He only hoped Rawlins was in position on the rear and could take out the snipers from that direction. If not, it didn't look good.

Factor in the four large, grim-faced gunmen near the bench, digging inside overcoats and pulling out hardware, and the list of unforeseen problems kept multiplying. As long as he was breathing, though, survival was never a long shot to Bolan.

"You people blink again, your boy here is the first to catch a bullet," Calhoun snarled over his shoulder.

"How dare you!" Santiago roared. "This is an outrage!"

"I told you to shut up!"

Two mini-Uzis and two handguns were brandished by Santiago's henchmen. They checked their fire, uncertain.

Bolan was grimly aware that it was about to hit the fan. But facing death was nothing new. Targets were many, and it would take some fast, lethal shooting to bail himself out. Then, out of the corner of his eye, he caught a fleeting glimpse of another trio of shadows to his left flank. Now he was pinched in a potential cross fire, with snipers to the north and south. Clearly Calhoun had stalled long enough to get his kill teams ready.

"So, you want my head on a platter?" Calhoun called out. "You're going to be a tough guy, is that it, soldier?"

Bicyclists rolled past Bolan. They glanced back at the standoff, the visible hardware, and biked on at a quicker pace. Any second the Executioner knew park police could show up. It wasn't beneath Calhoun, he knew, to gun down NYPD officers if they got in his way.

"You're going out of business, Calhoun," Bolan said. Shoving his prisoner to the side, the soldier reached out and reeled in Abu.

The Palestinian struggled and cried out in anger, but

Bolan growled in his ear, "Try to run, and you're the first to die on this side."

"You won't leave here alive, American," Abu said.

"If I don't make it, you don't, either," Bolan promised.

"Morrow, Hurley, back down and walk to me," Calhoun called out. "If Santiago's people make a move, cut loose."

"You're insane, Calhoun!" Santiago said. "Our business is finished. My people—"

"I don't need you to conclude my deal. You're just an errand boy for the cartel. You're so stupid, you don't even know how expendable you are."

Bolan was certain Calhoun's snipers were pros, with plenty of combat experience to back them up. One expertly placed head shot, and Bolan knew he was finished. It was reaching critical mass. Now that Calhoun ordered his men out of the line of fire, Bolan expected to feel bullets tearing into him any second. Initially he figured he might have walked into a drug deal and Calhoun had men there to cover the meet in case it soured for whatever reason. Then again Bolan read an arrogance in Calhoun's stare that told him he'd been expected all along, that his death was exactly what the former Special Forces major had designed. And Calhoun firmly believed he could kill everyone there and walk on.

Shooting his way out was now the only option, Bolan realized. The only winners here would be the survivors—the quickest gun, the most savage determination, not to mention a little luck. Abu and Afil were nothing more to Bolan than human shields meant to absorb the opening rounds. They were terrorists who had taken untold innocent lives. Life was as cheap to them as it was to Calhoun. Their numbers were up.

It would be tricky and it would take some lightning-fast footwork, but Bolan knew he had no choice but to use them to save his neck and hope to make cover off the trail. To his side there was a scattering of maples, set apart like prongs. If he could make the tree cover, he might be shielded from sniper cross fire.

Calhoun's men slowly drew a pair of Ingram MAC-10s. They held the weapons low by their sides as they backed up into the clearing, angling for position on the flanks of Santiago's henchmen. At the moment it was a standoff.

"O'Malley gave me enough to unravel your operation." It was a bluff, but the soldier was playing any angle he could. If he antagonized Calhoun, he might learn something.

"The guy didn't have squat on me. Second you don't have a clue as to what this is really about."

"I'm giving you a way out, Calhoun," Bolan said. Offering the man an option to surrender was a ridiculous stretch, but Bolan was stalling for time, hoping Rawlins was in position, had spotted the sniper teams and was ready to make a move on at least one of his covered flanks.

"To do what? Squawk before a bunch of pencil pushers on some Senate committee? I don't know who the hell you are or what your game is, but let me tell you something. This thing is bigger than you or me. You think you can roll up my flanks with your double-header last night, but you haven't even scratched my reserves. You think you can roll right in here, stones as big as avocados, granted, take me out and that will end it? Even if you dropped me, ten more are ready to take my place. Who I work for and what I am involved in is bigger than you or anybody else can possibly fathom."

"Consider me in the dark. What is it you're after?"

"Justice in a world gone mad. I'm a front-line soldier for a new world order. Enough said."

Calhoun had the rabid look of the fanatic Bolan had seen countless times. The man was beyond reason, but at least the soldier could now clearly see what he was dealing with.

Abu began to shake with rage. "I am beginning to see just how expendable I am to you, Major. You never intended to deal justly with myself or my men. We were simply tools for you to use."

"What's he planned, Abu?" Bolan asked. "You might as well tell me. He doesn't give a damn if you live or die."

"He is going to attack Manhattan!"

"How? When?"

With everyone locked in on his own agenda, it was bound to explode. Calhoun cursed Abu. Santiago began to rise, yelling obscenities in Spanish. Bolan met Calhoun's gaze, caught what he judged as a flicker of treachery in the man's eyes, then heard the enemy say, "We're walking out of here."

It was the raised note in Calhoun's voice, the glance to his flanks that warned Bolan the moment was upon him.

Calhoun snatched Santiago close to him, wheeled and joined his two gunmen in cutting loose on the Colombian's security team. It was a triple lightning burst from stammering weapons that caught the four-man security force by surprise, freezing them long enough for Calhoun and his killers to get the upper hand.

Bolan made his move. First to save himself, then to fight back with all he had.

Whipping out the Uzi, the Executioner shrank between Abu and Afil as whispering lead snapped the air around him. Caught off guard, perhaps still clinging to the belief that Calhoun would somehow deal straight with them or bail them out, the Arabs froze and bore the lethal impact of the opening rounds. Grabbing Afil, Bolan hurled the Palestinian in front of him as blood sprayed over his head and both terrorists screamed and jerked under the impacts. The human wall was quickly ventilated by converging streams of lead.

On the fly as Abu and Afil pitched to the trail, Bolan nose-dived between the maples. Bark flayed his face, then he caught a sharp cry of pain. Uphill he glimpsed one of the snipers tumbling down the slope. The darting shadow of Rawlins was all the soldier needed to see as the agent flew in on the hill snipers' flank, his compact Ingram chugging out whispering lead and pinning down those gunmen.

From the bench area, Calhoun, using Santiago as a shield, held back on the trigger of his Ingram. At close range Calhoun and his gunmen mowed down the Colombians, who stood their turf and tried to fire back. In the wild spray of bullets, Santiago took a direct hit in the chest. With utter shock as his death mask, the Colombian diplomat flopped like a rag doll in Calhoun's embrace. Taking Santiago's blood in the face, the ex-major poured it on. One final hosing of the security force, then Calhoun turned his Ingram toward Bolan, spinning his human armor. Beside Calhoun, the Colombians were doing a weird tap dance as cloth and flesh kept exploding and blood flew. One by one they dropped beneath the lead hurricane.

On the run, as bullets chewed up bark, Bolan primed a fragmentation grenade. One chance was all he would get. Left-handed he hosed a stream of 9 mm slugs at the snipers to the south. One sniper triggered his silenced Ingram from the cover of a boulder while he was flanked by two other grim-faced shadows firing from behind trees. A raking burst of Uzi fire, and Bolan sent them to cover long enough for him to lob the metal egg.

They came up, firing, just as the grenade bounced against the boulder. It blew, catching the snipers by complete surprise. Bolan heard a scream, glimpsed a man clutching his face from the blast of countless steel fragments, and launched backward, but he was already darting for deeper cover. By now Calhoun had tossed away Santiago's lifeless body as if the dead Colombian were nothing more than a sack of garbage.

As Bolan heard Calhoun order a retreat, he squeezed off a quick burst when the ex-major bounded over the bench. The soldier scored only wood, then was forced to duck as the two gunmen from that fire zone covered their leader with long bursts.

Whatever the treacherous former major was after, it was big enough for him to risk it all in this moment of insanity. That it had blown up in one instant of killing ferocity didn't surprise Bolan.

The Executioner checked his flank. The south snipers had moved on. Down the trail, the two surviving snipers emerged. One of them had come up on a young male jogger who had blundered into the killing zone. The gunman had grabbed the civilian around the throat.

Crouched low, braving the lead that ate bark to his back, Bolan nailed the other sniper with a 3-round burst to the chest. The gunman was hurled back, triggering a final burst from his weapon before he skidded down the trail.

Covered by his two gunners, Calhoun was already melting into the woods off the clearing.

Bolan wanted Calhoun finished on the spot, but knew he was losing the edge. Survival came first for the soldier. If Calhoun lived to carry on whatever his warped fight was, Bolan would dog him, no matter where he went.

The Executioner fixed his sights on the lone sniper who was sidling across the trail, his human shield writhing in his grasp. Snapping off a clean shot was risky, but Bolan intended to see the civilian live. He lowered his aim and went for an exposed knee of his enemy when he got a clear line of fire.

The gunman pulled his Ingram away from the civilian's temple and was set to fire when his world turned to instant agony.

Bolan cut loose with the Uzi. As the gunner's bone shattered, he toppled. The jogger tried to flee, stumbled, then leaped to his feet.

Either incensed by Bolan's turning the tide and flinging it in his face, or acting in mindless rage and agony, the gunman managed to roll up on a leg, then caught the jogger in the back with a stuttering barrage of bullets. The jogger was dead before he hammered to the trail on his face. Bolan took instant vengeance for the senseless butchering of the innocent and nailed the wounded gunman with the last four rounds in his clip.

Gunfire tore back at Bolan's cover. He hugged the tree, then filled the Uzi with a fresh clip. Relentless subgun fire held Bolan in check. Stuttering rounds seemed to blaze over his position, on and on. An eternity later there was a sudden lull. Bolan peered low around his cover.

Calhoun and his killers were suddenly nowhere to be found.

Frustrated, Bolan checked the vicinity. He was alone

right then with the dead. Anyone witnessing the firefight from a distance had most likely fled. Soon police would be converging on the killzone.

Running, combat senses still on full alert but knowing Calhoun was gone, Bolan was moving up the slope when a hideous groan snared his attention. Beside him, outstretched near a tree, he spotted the bloodied form of Rawlins.

From the top of the rise he searched the wooded area below. Two figures appeared in the distance, then surged through an underpass. He had lost Calhoun, and he wouldn't further risk a running gun battle through Central Park. One innocent was already dead, and it was obvious Calhoun would use unknowing victims to save himself. If luck prevailed on Calhoun's side, Bolan figured the enemy gunners would keep their heads low, walk right out. Most likely Calhoun had a contingency plan, a team ready to meet him with a vehicle in the park and whisk him safely away.

Wiping blood off his face with the back of his hand, Bolan strode toward Rawlins. He saw the agent had taken several rounds to the chest. The way the man was wheezing, with blood bubbling on his lips, Bolan knew a round or two had found lung.

With a shaky hand, Rawlins dug a piece of paper from his pants pocket. "My people...are dead. Address... directions...don't...ask questions."

Bolan took the slip of paper. Rawlins coughed blood. "Under the toilet lid...anything they got...take it...Calhoun has...to be...stopped..."

Life faded from the agent's eyes on a death rattle.

Not wasting another moment, Bolan rose to retrace his path out of the park. Time was running out. At least the Executioner had another starting place, even if he was still clueless as to what was staged for Manhattan. Perhaps dead men did talk.

NO ONE SPOKE until they were in the Lincoln Tunnel and rolling for their command center in New Jersey.

"That bastard moved quick," Morrow growled.

"I nailed Goatee, but I couldn't confirm if any other dogs were on our heels," the short, crew-cut Sampson said. "Big guy is a pro, assessed the situation and used our two boys to bail himself out. I didn't factor that action in."

"They were acting on their own, gentlemen," Calhoun stated.

"I hope Abu's boys don't get cold feet now that he's out of the game, Major," Billerton said.

"Abu only has two complete units out of the twenty," Augustly commented. "We can still move without his people."

Calhoun wiped blood off his face with the towel. Hunched on the seat in the back of the van, he scoured the faces of Morrow, Billerton and Augustly. Augustly made a good point, Calhoun knew.

Luckily the terrorist army they had trained and fielded was comprised of enough different fanatics from various countries that Abu wouldn't even be mentioned. And why should he? Whether they were Iraqis, Syrians, Palestinians or Jordanians they all carried the same rabid desire to kill Americans. Violent death was always expected among their rank and file, even actively sought in their jihad. It was their common bond of going out in a blaze of glory for God that Calhoun had always used and now counted on. From the beginning he had never expected to lay eyes on any of them again after his New York mission. Of course, money had been promised if they lived, but many of them were so hell-bent on striking their glorious blow to America, the Great Satan, that it was all Calhoun could do to keep them from charging ahead too soon.

Shortly each team would be contacted, given the order. Everything was timing. Even if only half of the twenty units were successful, it would still bring utter chaos and mayhem, terror and death to the island of Manhattan. How many would die in the coming slaughter was up to the determination and fanaticism of the terrorist army.

Mentally Calhoun assessed the present damage. Peterswythe, Johnson, Clickert and Bobstill. KIA. Four good soldiers, with him since Vietnam and the Company's black operations into Laos and Cambodia. More ghosts now, gone to the graveyard of bitter memory.

They were dead, and he was still alive and free to carry on. Somehow the rest of them had melted into the crowd near the zoo. As fate would have it, a flurry of mounted and foot police had swept a trail, far behind them, five minutes after fleeing the killzone, not even glancing in their direction. Montain, now driving, had picked them up as they made their way down East Drive. Of course, if anyone had tried to stop them on the way out, Calhoun and his men would have shot first without blinking. If they had evaded confrontation in that manner, it was possible the big guy with the Uzi could have done just the same. Calhoun put the unknown opposition out of mind. Before long New York would be a memory. And they would have shown their sponsors just how capable they were at commanding troops who could enact an all-out siege.

Calhoun saw Montain looking in the side mirror. "Problem, Mr. Montain?"

"No, sir. Just checking."

"The tape?" Calhoun asked.

Montain reached beneath the seat and pulled out a videotape. Calhoun took it as Montain said, "Went off like clockwork, sir. Should keep the police busy all morning."

The van itself was a rolling command center. Calhoun took the tape and slid it into the small TV-VCR. In the rear of the van, Billerton had on the radio headset, monitoring all police frequencies with his scanner.

"Anything to report?"

"All police activity is confined to the park and the Upper West Side vicinity. Doesn't sound as if they have any descriptions of us, sir. It would appear the opening round was a success, Major."

"Raise the general, Lieutenant Billerton," Calhoun ordered. "We pull out as soon as the operation is under way. I want a full security detail of six men around the perimeter of the command center."

"Aye, aye, Major."

Intent, Calhoun watched the image snap to life on the compact screen. He saw a limousine in front of a white stone building. The image flickered to static for a moment, then the limo came back a heartbeat before it went up in a fireball. The picture abruptly died.

"I've got all of three seconds, Mr. Montain," Calhoun rasped. "What the hell happened? It couldn't even confirm the targets."

"Our man on-site confirmed the kill of the Israeli diplomat and his envoy, sir. Apparently our operative became nervous as he was too close to the scene. He ended visual transmission without warning or on order. He was met thirty minutes later by Captain Shingles and paid in full as previously ordered."

That was good enough for Calhoun. When he had learned from Abu that the terrorist had long ago infiltrated one of their own into the security detail and targeted the Israeli diplomatic envoy, Calhoun had made the concession to work out the details with the Palestinian in exchange for further cooperation for the New York mission. It was, of course, only a small beginning of what the city was about to taste.

Calhoun looked at Billerton. "Raise each unit, Lieutenant. I want them in synch and ready to go on my order. I also want no unit to end visual or audio transmission unless I give the order."

Calhoun checked his watch. Sixty minutes and counting.

Less than an hour away, Manhattan would catch a glimpse of doomsday. And if any of the terrorists managed to survive and escape the conflagration they would unleash, they, like the operative who had planted the C-4 on the limo of the Israeli diplomat, would be paid in full.

One bullet each.

10

Supposedly the man bringing the final payment was the most feared assassin the KGB had ever trained and put into the field. Aleksandr Nikoly, formerly a colonel in the Soviet Union's special forces, known as Spetsnaz, had only met Petre Kuschka once. Since then, many terrible stories about Kuschka had circulated among Nikoly's comrades in the GRU, the Soviet military intelligence. It was rumored that Kuschka had killed at least a thousand men, either by gun, knife or with his bare hands. It was told that Kuschka would sometimes decapitate his victims if the target was of "special interest" to his KGB superiors. Rumor or truth, Nikoly knew either way he still had much to fear from the former KGB man.

Walking from his desk, Nikoly slipped into his insulated parka. He shivered, wondered if it was the thought of venturing outside into the subzero air of his temporary and remote Siberian outpost, or the recollection of the lifeless black eyes of a stone-cold killer. Memory now haunted him.

It had been a strange and sordid affair. Outside Kabul, during the fiasco of the war in Afghanistan, they had met during a joint KGB-Spetsnaz operation. Drinking vodka over a shipment of opium, to be delivered to what had become the Russian Mafia, Nikoly recalled how they had passionately discussed the future of Mother Russia.

Nikoly and Kuschka drew one absolute conclusion— money would soon become the only god to the Soviet hordes who foolishly craved to become like the decadent West. Simply put, if they couldn't beat the system, join it—at least until they acquired, through bribery and graft, enough influence to back them up for a revolution down the road.

So the future for glasnost had been paved, to some degree, by Nikoly's war profiteering with the assassin from the KGB's Thirteenth Directorate. Only what precisely was Kuschka's ultimate goal, Nikoly never found out. Huge sums of money were made during their brief but lucrative pact with the fledgling Russian criminal organization.

The Afghan war eventually ended, Kuschka disappeared and Nikoly went on with his life as a colonel in Spetsnaz. After their lone encounter, Nikoly spent years hoping Kuschka would never enter his life again. There was something so deadly and so predatory about the KGB man that Nikoly often imagined, even years later, he was still holding a poisonous serpent by the tail for ever having even met the man one time.

His fear had become reality.

Striding from his barracks, flipping up the hood on his white parka, the short, stocky Nikoly searched the black skies over the Siberian tundra. Toting AK-47s, three ex-Spetsnaz soldiers trailed Nikoly across the frozen, snow-packed compound grounds, which were bathed in the white glare from floodlights. West, Nikoly spotted the giant shape of the Ilyushin Il-76 as it banked, then descended for landing.

Nikoly gave the bleak wooden buildings of the compound a quick once-over. All present had been ordered out of their barracks. Thirty-three ex-Spetsnaz soldiers with AK-47s, slung across their shoulders, were exiting the buildings.

Looking around at the transport trucks, the giant satellite dish and fuel drums, the entire perimeter ringed by barbed-wired fences, Nikoly felt a heavy weight settle on his shoulders. To even be there was depressing.

Long ago the compound had been a gulag but was converted to a secret training base for Spetsnaz. Then the compound had been shut down in the wake of glasnost and the new regime of money-grubbing bureaucrats who were content to watch Russia collapse under the guise of democracy while they fattened their pockets. A part of Nikoly ached for the old days when there was law and order, even if it came from the barrel of a gun. Fortunately there were still many hard-line Communists behind the scenes who were prepared to restore Mother Russia to the old ways. When that happened, Nikoly believed he should be in another country, spending his illicit earnings. He was getting too old for rebellion.

The transport plane landed between the rows of lights, rolled on the permafrost, which was as hard as concrete. Clouds of white spumed in the wake of the gigantic transport plane. It struck Nikoly that Kuschka was far more powerful, with far more connections in the right places, than he had at first realized. Not just any ex-KGB operative could command an Ilyushin and fly the airspace over Siberia at will. Nikoly wondered just how deep and far the conspiracy reached.

Whatever, the past had been resurrected when a liaison from Kuschka's arrived at Nikoly's Moscow apartment. The ominous discussion, six months earlier, had been brief but rife with subtle hints of blackmail. If Nikoly didn't arrange for Kuschka to buy a mercenary army of Spetsnaz soldiers who had been under the colonel's command in Afghanistan, there could be dire consequences.

Growing old, tired, his wife dead and his children grown and gone, Nikoly came out of semiretirement. Using his contacts in the GRU, he had managed to track down and offer wealth beyond anyone's dreams to men who were once soldiers of the highest caliber. Of course, Kuschka had sent a down payment, to be returned, naturally, if the soldiers the KGB assassin wanted weren't found or convinced to enlist in his revolutionary army. Exactly what the former KGB assassin had in mind, Nikoly didn't know. But he suspected the future held a revolution unlike anything in the history of Russia.

Nikoly and his soldiers cleared the front gate. They strode to the edge of the airstrip as the aircraft taxied to a stop. The mercenary army spread out and stood at attention. Nikoly shivered, waited. A low wind howled in from the endless steppe.

Finally a tall figure in a black leather trench coat appeared.

At first, Kuschka appeared like a wraith, as long strides carried him through the settling mist of snow and the glare of lights. Closing, he became an unnerving sight to Nikoly: thick, bushy eyebrows over the same coal black eyes he remembered; the face long, as sharp as an ax, cheekbones high and jaw square. There were scars on the man's forehead he didn't remember from before. Probably inflicted, he guessed, from shrapnel flaying his face from some distant killing field. With his silver hair swept back to reveal another jagged scar along the temple, Kuschka presented a formidable picture of a man who had survived many life-or-death encounters.

A dozen figures in white parkas, AK-47s slung around their shoulders, trailed the ex-KGB killer. Nikoly noted the troops lugged six large duffel bags. Kuschka and Nikoly gave each other a curt nod.

"Comrade Nikoly. It has been a long time. I am glad you made the right decision."

"I believe I was in no position to do otherwise, Comrade."

"Sometimes the choice is made for men such as us."

As Kuschka nodded over his shoulder, five of the duffel bags were opened. They bulged with U.S. dollars. Briefly Nikoly wondered why the sixth bag wasn't unzipped.

Gently Kuschka tugged Nikoly away from the troops. "Ten million in American, as we agreed, Comrade Nikoly. Half is with me, and the other half has been electronically wired to a bank in a country I will disclose to you in time."

Nikoly tensed but kept his expression blank. "I do not understand, Comrade. I have done what you asked. I went to great trouble, even risked my life to find the men you asked for. I have been removed from Moscow by your people and placed here in the middle of somewhere I can only describe as the ends of the earth. I am even afraid to return to Moscow for fear I have become a hunted criminal."

"Your efforts will not go unrewarded. I will need you to stay here for another few days. I will send someone who will stay with you until some matters are cleared up and I feel it is safe for you to return to Moscow or leave the country."

"I do not understand. What is it you could possibly still need me to do?"

"In time you will know. You must continue to remain loyal and unquestioning. And, I must mention, useful."

Nikoly felt his heart sink. Instinct warned him he was a dead man when he had served whatever purpose Kuschka intended for him. Another part of him clung to the hope he wouldn't be executed as a way for Kuschka to cover his tracks.

"Now," Kuschka said, "I must address my troops."

Nikoly watched as Kuschka slowly walked back to the chosen thirty-three. Grim, breath pluming out of his nostrils in the frigid air, he examined each face, peering into each set of eyes. None of the men selected acknowledged his scrutiny or even blinked.

"Comrades," Kuschka began, "I will be blunt. You have made the only decision possible. You were selected by myself for a reason, and your purpose for what lies ahead is far greater than you could imagine. I know each and every one of you, from the day you were born, to your impeccable service records to your shabby lives beyond Spetsnaz.

"You were once dedicated, loyal, highly disciplined and combat-seasoned soldiers who served the motherland without question, without fail. That was yesterday. Today, I have pulled you from the gutters of alcoholism, divorce, unemployment and shattered family life. Some of you have even tried your hands at minor criminal activity. Drug dealing, gambling, pimping. No more."

Kuschka cleared his throat, his jaw clenched with determination. "Comrades, you are now standing in the middle of what is called Siberia. This frozen wasteland makes up half of our Mother Russia, but holds only nine percent of our population because of its inhospitable nature. All around you, reaching for as far as the eye can see, is a landscape that could yield more wealth in the form of coal, natural gas, oil, diamonds and other precious metals than perhaps any place on this planet. Why do I mention this seemingly trivial bit of information? It is because like this land, you men also have great and untapped reserves of wealth, but in the form of a warrior's spirit. You, like this land, will someday know your full potential.''

Nikoly felt a dark and angry depression welling inside. Essentially they were told they were all expendable, meat on a hook. "Potential" meant what they could do for Kuschka and whatever he had planned. These men were better off dead. Nikoly began feeling enormous regret. Greed had seized him, years ago, in Kabul. Never once had his family seen a dime of his ill-gotten gain. He had deluded himself, and now he might as well have been put in front of a firing squad. Kuschka was insane.

Kuschka glanced around, then continued. "In short, you will see me as your savior, one who can cleanse you and restore you to your former glory. That untapped wealth, Comrades. You have been paid to perform a service for your country even if your country is unaware you are on the threshold of history, answering the call to save us all. You freely accepted my offer and my money. You will now serve me, or you will die.''

Nikoly became more uncomfortable with each passing moment. He felt the eyes of the ex-KGB troops boring into him. He glanced at the lone bag in the snow. It was impossible to even guess its contents. Looking back at Kuschka, Nikoly found the former assassin's eyes were lit with a sudden and savage intensity.

"In time you will be thoroughly briefed on what is expected of you," Kuschka went on, raising his voice, hands clasped behind his back, pivoting and striding back up the line. "I will say this much. With the coming of a new century, a new order, a new age will dawn. Not only for Russia, but for the entire world. As we speak, it has already begun. Now, we will be working with Westerners who at this very moment, halfway around the world, are proving they will be useful in launching the new age. Cultural and philosophical differences, all prejudice must be put aside. Only the most brilliant minds, the strongest of warriors, the purest and the most determined of wills can prevail in the time ahead.

"You will once again become killing machines in flesh. You will be working beside soldiers from many different nations. Indeed, the task ahead of you is formidable, but the survival of Russia and the world is at stake, Comrades. You will be fed, housed and well paid and, of course, retrained. Should you fail me or disobey me, you will be shot where you stand. However, should you survive what is ahead for all of us, you will be part of a glory the world has yet to see."

Nikoly watched as Kuschka nodded at one of his troops. The man bent and zipped open the last duffel bag. When he saw what was inside, Nikoly grimaced, his heart racing with fear. At least three pairs of unseeing eyes stared up from the bag. The man kicked the bag. A severed head rolled out and rested a few feet from Nikoly in the snow.

"Perhaps, Comrades," Kuschka said, and smiled, "you have heard stories of my exploits. If you have heard rumors, I bring you proof that what you heard was fact." Kuschka glared at the dead faces, then glowered at the lone head. "Those men were intelligence officers of the GRU, men who formerly controlled you. They were following me, and I found out they wished to obstruct my goal. If I even think a man wishes to betray me, that is how he will end up.''

Nikoly met the former assassin's cold stare. A smile cut Kuschka's lips, then he ordered, "I want everyone boarded within the next five minutes. Dismissed.''

The ex-commandos moved for their barracks to gather their gear. Within five minutes Nikoly would be utterly alone on the Siberian outpost. One of the ex-KGB men picked up and tossed a money bag, which landed beside Nikoly. The troops seized every bag except the one Nikoly wished they would take the most. A warning, or a vision of his own future?

"I will contact you with further instructions,'' Kuschka said, then wheeled and strode for the transport plane.

Again Aleksandr Nikoly regretted ever having laid eyes on Kuschka. He wondered if even years ago the man had staged this very moment.

It was too late now for regrets. Nikoly knew there was no way out.

11

There was only one way in. As far as the Executioner was concerned, time was running out, and he knew he had to kick the blitz into high gear. Unknown disaster was waiting in Manhattan. But at the moment, he needed to clean up unfinished business on the Jersey side of the Hudson River.

Having retrieved his rental vehicle, Bolan pulled up at the front gate to Styx Security and Trucking.

The Executioner had made good time since putting behind the carnage in Central Park. Earlier he had walked right out of the park, alert for anyone, lawmen or enemy, who might blindside him. With all the confusion, Bolan simply melted into crowd. Sirens had wailed up and down Fifth Avenue and beyond. Shrinking into the moving throngs on the sidewalk, he had witnessed a swarm of uniformed policemen surging for the entrance at Central Park South.

Now the soldier was looking for a lead to pick up the trail on Calhoun. He would settle up with Sternmann, find the cache of weapons—if it was on the grounds of the warehouse—and destroy it. As far as Bolan was concerned, Sternmann was as dirty as Calhoun. Behind the facade of legitimate business, the man was moving guns, destined to fall into the hands of criminals. And it appeared Sternmann also hired out former military men as professional killers.

Once grim business was concluded here, Bolan would make his way back to the address near Times Square and find out just what Rawlins's colleagues had left behind, if anything. And if nothing else, he would be putting himself in the general vicinity of whatever Calhoun had designed for Manhattan. It was a long shot to track down any terrorists Calhoun would unleash, but Bolan intended to position himself on the front line somehow. All he could really do was wait for the terrorists to strike.

The large sign over the front gate announced Bolan had arrived at the right place; Brognola's directions to the warehouse tucked at the edge of an industrial park in Hoboken proved accurate.

A guard sprang out of the small booth, his expression surly. Beneath the guy's jacket, Bolan spotted the bulge of a weapon. Suspicious, the man scowled at Bolan, but the soldier was out of the vehicle, Beretta unleathered and thrust in the man's face. If Bolan's hunch was right, Sternmann would have a few goons on hand, packing hardware and ready to defend the merchandise on the grounds.

Bolan didn't see any cameras on the chain-link fence or on the booth. If his luck held, he could surprise the owner.

"What is this?" the guard asked.

"Where's Sternmann?"

"Who the hell are you?"

Bolan shoved the man back into the booth. The warehouse appeared every bit as large as the one he had destroyed in the Bronx. Across the lot he counted at least ten 18-wheelers parked in respective loading bays. A few workers bustled about the docks, and a forklift moved pallets heaped with crates.

"I'm getting tired of you answering questions with a question," the soldier growled. "Last chance. Where can I find your boss?"

"Far north end, down the alley. Door is marked office."

"Thanks," Bolan said, then knocked the guard unconscious with a slashing right. He took the guard's .45 Colt.

Bolan slid behind the wheel and rolled onto the grounds. Anyone brandishing a weapon was fair game. It was possible some people who worked for Sternmann were civilians, perhaps unaware of what their boss shipped out. Bolan would call it on the spot.

No one showed in Bolan's path as he drove down an alley that separated Sternmann property from another undetermined building. He parked beside the marked door, got out and scanned the alley in both directions.

Unwatched at the moment, Bolan drew his silenced Beretta. He tried the door handle and found it unlocked. Crouched low, the soldier bulldozed into the office. Just in case a gunman was waiting on the other side, Bolan hit the deck and rolled across the floor. Coming up, he saw a big man with a neatly trimmed beard and mustache rise from behind a metal desk. A large-caliber pistol came into Bolan's view, but he was already snapping off a 9 mm round. The big guy yelped in pain as the slug tore into his arm, and he pitched into the filing cabinets behind the desk.

Bolan closed the door behind him, Beretta fanning the small office. He heard the man groaning in pain, saw the top of a balding pate. The .357 Magnum pistol the guy had intended to use was lying useless on the floor beside the desk.

"On your feet," the Executioner ordered. "Are you Sternmann?"

"Yeah! Who are you?"

"A problem from the Bronx as of last night."

Fear broke through the pain in Sternmann's eyes as the man clutched his bloodied arm.

Bolan trained the Beretta on the man. "I'm looking for a certain truck delivered to you by Ben Calhoun."

"I don't know what you're talking about."

The Beretta sneezed, drilling into metal beside Sternmann's face. "Wrong answer. Last chance. I want a truck that is loaded with weapons you purchased from Calhoun."

"Okay, okay. It's the only one in the warehouse."

A heartbeat later Bolan discovered why the answer came so easy. A burly figure burst through a door beside a table holding computers and a fax machine. The guy charged in hard, was drawing a bead on Bolan with a stubby Ingram MAC-10 when Bolan shot him square between the eyes. Death throes carried the gunman into the wall, his finger squeezing back on the trigger long enough to clip off a burst that turned a computer into sparking ruins. The shots could have also alerted other hardmen.

Time to move and turn up the heat.

Bolan was all over Sternmann in three long strides. Sternmann had nearly grabbed up the pistol when Bolan kicked him in his wounded arm.

The man cursed viciously as the Executioner hauled him to his feet. Jamming the Beretta's sound suppressed muzzle into Sternmann's ear, Bolan said, "We're taking a walk. We'll talk on the way. Anybody gets cute, you're dead before you hit the ground.''

Holding Sternmann tight, Bolan took the keys, went to his vehicle and opened the trunk. He hauled out the satchel of C-4 and hung it across his shoulder. One eye on his rear, Bolan asked, ''You hit an alarm buzzer under your desk when I came?''

Scowling, Sternmann answered, ''Yeah.''

''Understand that when we go into the warehouse, you're my armor against anyone who gets trigger-happy.''

''What is it you want?''

Bolan found they were still alone as he shoved Sternmann up the alley. ''Answers. Where can I find Calhoun?''

''I don't know, and that's the truth.''

''What is Calhoun after?''

''Look, I knew the guy in Vietnam. We were part of a covert CIA operation called Scorpion. Behind-the-lines spook stuff.''

''Wet work.''

''Whatever. A lot of things went sour. I was part of a special unit that Calhoun commanded. Twice we were hung out to dry by our own people. Bottom line, I think it pushed Calhoun over the edge. He started running guns to the other side in exchange for heroin.''

''Sounds like he carried on well for himself all these years.''

''Calhoun resurfaced about a year ago. My business was failing. The guy made an offer to get me back on my feet.''

''He used you. Specifically to infiltrate his own professional killers into your business to then work as security people for targets he wanted eliminated. I know about Muldare. I was there last night when O'Malley was killed. I was the only one who made it out.''

Bolan tugged Sternmann around the corner. From the loading bays, a few workmen were milling around the 18-wheelers. If the brief sound of gunfire had warned them of trouble, it didn't show by the way they casually went on with their business. Even still, Bolan knew the alert had been sounded. Perhaps there were only a few gunners inside the warehouse. Maybe they kept hardware out of sight, not wanting to intimidate the workmen.

''Look, whoever you are, most of these guys are just dumb civs.''

''But some carry automatic weapons. You're a man with a lot to hide and protect. Keep talking to me. Your life depends on it. How does Calhoun get in touch with you?''

''By phone or fax.''

''When was the last time you heard from the man?''

''This morning. First the phone. He told me about the problem it turns out you created in the Bronx. Then I get a fax. He wants the rest of his payment for the shipment of weapons.''

''To buy a large supply of drugs?''

''I'm sure that's part of what he does.''

''And imports terrorism to America.''

''I wouldn't know about that, but with him anything is possible.''

Bolan was getting the impression Sternmann knew very little about Calhoun's agenda outside the weapons dealing. But he hoped Sternmann would provide him with a lead.

''Out of curiosity, how much do you owe Calhoun?''

''Three million.''

"Is he coming to you or sending someone to pick it up?"

"No," Sternmann said. "I'm supposed to go to Miami right away with his money. No later than nine tomorrow morning."

"Sounds like you're short."

"I have enough to stall him."

"It doesn't matter. Calhoun's going out of business. You have a decision to make. Go to Miami with me, or I travel alone. Where in Miami?"

"A place in North Miami Beach—1542 Oceanfront Drive." He then told Bolan the standing order was to go into the house, which would be left unlocked, and wait for someone to show.

"It wasn't supposed to be this way," Sternmann rasped.

"Maybe you haven't heard. Crime doesn't pay."

"A few shipments of guns, that's all. They were going to dope dealers and drug gangs. Money delivered, merchandise dropped off. Clean and simple."

"You didn't factor in one thing."

"What?"

"Me."

Sternmann grunted. "I don't even like Calhoun, mister. He's crazy as the day is long. Years back he was always raving about how the world screwed him over. Now it's how the world is going to end, all civilization as we know it will perish when the barbarians storm the gates, unless a few good men stand up and stop the savage hordes. That's pretty much a quote. I swear to you, I have no idea what the crazy bastard really intends."

"You were just in it for the money."

"What else?"

"As much as you hold Calhoun in fear and contempt, all you did was become just like him. Do you know how many lives the weapons you ship out will take? Innocent lives, caught in the cross fire of thugs who, like you, are just in it for the money."

"That's not my problem."

"It is now."

The workers finally looked up as Bolan closed the gap, guiding his hostage down the loading dock. They froze, confused and startled.

"I would find a new employer when you leave here. You men have thirty seconds to clear the premises," Bolan said. They hesitated. "Now you have twenty-eight. Do you need a jolt of reality like your boss?"

It took only one glance at the blood pouring from Sternmann's wound, and they scattered for the parking lot.

Bolan then made Sternmann give the order for all present inside the warehouse to clear out. Again the workers didn't move fast enough. Bolan counted ten men, give or take. None of them looked armed.

Inspiration for the work crew to bolt appeared around the corner of a pile of crates.

The guy popped into view with an Uzi, drew a bead on Bolan but checked his fire when he saw his boss shielding the intruder. The savage determination in the gunman's eyes warned Bolan he was looking for an opening to cut loose, a leg shot, a kneecapper, anything. Not taking any chances, Bolan shot him in the chest, flung him down the aisle under the whispering impact of sudden death. Above, on the north catwalk, another Uzi gunner reared up.

"Don't shoot!" Sternmann cried.

By now employees were scurrying from the warehouse. Bolan shoved his Beretta in Sternmann's ear.

"Drop it now, down on the floor!" Bolan ordered. "Hands up and on your knees."

Reluctantly the gunman sent his weapon clattering off the warehouse floor.

"How many in here are armed?"

"Three. Now two."

"You're telling the truth, right?"

"I'm betting my life on it, pal."

That left one unaccounted for. Out of the corner of his eye, Bolan then spotted the last hardman, armed with an Ingram, and wheeling around the corner to his other flank. Distracted for a split second, Bolan was too slow in reacting as Sternmann grabbed at his only chance to bail. The elbow hammered Bolan in the jaw. The soldier lost his hold on Sternmann, who ripped out of his grasp. The blow jarred Bolan to the bone. But even as stars exploded in his eyes, the sudden attack by his captive was the only thing that saved Bolan.

Stumbling back from the punishing blow, the Executioner pitched behind a forklift as autofire chattered. He gathered himself in the next instant. Crouched, he darted to the other side of the forklift as bullets whined off metal. Thinking he had Bolan pinned, the gunman scurried to the side, trying to angle for a better position. He triggered a short burst, raking the forklift. In his haste to gain an edge, the gunman's foot clipped the edge of a crate. Bolan finished off the man's tumble with a silent head shot.

Shots rang out from the catwalk. The gunman had pulled a pistol and was firing wildly. Bolan leathered the Beretta and unslung the Uzi. On the run, obviously catching sight of Bolan's hardware, the gunner dashed down the catwalk. If the guy thought he could outrun the Executioner's stream of 9 mm slugs, he was dead wrong. Bolan gave the gunman some lead, then blew him back through a window of an upstairs office.

Bolan listened as the echo of gunfire rattled around the warehouse. Outside, engines growled to life, and tires clawed at pavement.

Cautious, Bolan stepped away from the forklift. With no telling how many gunmen were in the warehouse, he was braced to shoot if necessary.

A gunman did wheel into his sights.

Sternmann had somehow gotten hold of an Ingram subgun. He got off a brief burst, but Bolan ended the man's short career as a criminal. Three bloody holes marched across Sternmann's chest as the impact of the slugs hurled him into a stack of crates.

For long moments Bolan listened for any sound of movement. Engine noise quickly died, silence hovered in the warehouse.

Senses electrified, Bolan peered inside the back of the 18-wheeler. He reached in and slid a heavy crate off the lip. When it hit the floor, Bolan pried off the lid with his combat knife.

Another payload of automatic weapons.

Quickly the Executioner went to work placing the C-4 charges.

IT WAS A REPEAT of the Bronx fireworks.

Bolan cleared the front gate. If the guard was still stretched out in the booth, he would shortly come to with a rude and terrifying awakening.

As it stood, Bolan drove on, unimpeded. The warehouse grounds looked clear of any signs of life. He checked his watch as the seconds ticked down on the time-delay charges he'd placed in the tractor trailer, and at strategic points around the warehouse to ensure total obliteration.

He gave the vehicle some gas, putting the industrial complex behind him. He heard the thunder, saw the fireball mushroom in his rearview mirror.

He had no more clear-cut answers than when he went in to Styx Security. If nothing else, Sternmann's business was up in flames, and Bolan may have saved a few lives with all the destruction blowing into the Hudson.

The Executioner was rolling on. It was back to Manhattan, and into more of the unknown.

12

Just as homicide detectives with no firm leads were often forced to wait for the serial killer to strike again, Bolan judged his situation in Manhattan to have hit a temporary wall. Even still, the Executioner never sat on the sidelines while the enemy lurked and plotted its next blow against innocents. For the time being, he was still mired in mystery, one hand tied behind his back, but he was searching for an option to jump-start the hunt for Calhoun.

Calhoun would resurface at some point. But where? When? And if the target was Manhattan, the list of potential strike points, with all the monuments, landmarks and skyscrapers, was endless and impossible for even an army of lawmen to cover.

At least the tape was where Rawlins had promised. And as the late agent had also told Bolan, the Company man's backup team was dead. How Rawlins knew they were dead was simply another nagging mystery. Perhaps they were supposed to check in with him at a scheduled time, or rendezvous. No contact may have signaled Rawlins the worst-case scenario had taken place.

Dropping the minicassette tape in his pocket, Bolan moved out into the living room. Two dead men: one stretched out on his back, a neat red hole between his eyes, the second operative slumped over the couch with likewise a third eye. Their Berettas were still tucked in their shoulder holsters. Somehow they were caught napping. Bolan could only make an educated guess as to what happened.

Their safehouse was a tacky efficiency unit in a building behind a porn stop off Forty-second Street. The adjacent bathroom or the closet could have hidden one, maybe two killers, waiting for the agents to return. Two lightning shots from a sound-suppressed weapon had ended their part of the operation. The place had been turned over, drawers opened, sofa cushions and bed mattress shredded by a sharp instrument, the few articles of clothing discarded. As if knowing the place was a risk for ransacking, it appeared they kept no listening devices, no clues as to who they were or what they had been doing. Haste, frustration or mere oversight had kept the killer from discovering the minicassette. More guesswork, of course, and Bolan had no more time to sift through all possibilities. What was done was done.

Bolan had two choices. Either call Brognola and have the man pull rank and put all law-enforcement agencies throughout the city on full alert, or move on to Miami. Option one was somewhat unrealistic, he concluded. First he had no clear fix on Calhoun's agenda. Sounding the alarm, with security heightened, the police and other law-enforcement agencies on standby could create a city-wide panic. Given the violence and mayhem of the past day, though, it was possible the mayor could be convinced to do everything short of declaring martial law. Besides, such a scenario was time-consuming. Bolan suspected it would be too late by then to thwart whatever terrorist act was designed for the city.

Something catastrophic was set to be launched anytime.

Heading to Miami sounded more feasible. First Bolan decided to get the cassette to Brognola. A short interlude at Stony Man Farm, going over whatever information the dead agents had learned with the Farm's computer experts, might prove fruitful. Then he could brief the big Fed and move on whatever intel was gathered on his enemies. Finally he could continue on to Miami to meet with Calhoun's pickup man, or another killing crew— whatever the case.

The way Bolan read the situation in Central Park, logic dictated Calhoun was holding hands with a major Colombian drug cartel. But the narcotics element, he still believed, was merely a small piece of the puzzle. From Miami, Colombia was next on the soldier's agenda.

With each violent or treacherous stop along the way, it increasingly became a question of climbing the ladder of riddles, a manhunt with a wait-and-see approach. Naturally it angered and frustrated Bolan the enemy was dictating the action right then, leaving him pretty much in the dark. At best he had damaged one or two ongoing operations the enemy had created in New York and New Jersey, shaved down some enemy numbers at Calhoun's disposal.

Small consolation.

Bolan glanced at the corpses. Hopefully they had given their lives if only to steer him in a direction where he could nail Calhoun before the traitor fulfilled whatever was on his agenda. If the CIA had some fix on Calhoun and his terrorist, drug and gunrunning operations, Bolan hoped Brognola could get him something through his own contacts at Langley to keep the trail hot.

Manhattan, though, was still a crapshoot. It was the

present unknown crisis Bolan kept himself concerned with.

Swiftly, intending to raise Brognola once he was back in his vehicle in the parking garage, Bolan headed out of the shabby apartment complex. Typical noise of horns blaring from the street, arguments in other complexes, television and loud music swirled around him as he ventured downstairs.

Before entering the safehouse, he had filled the Uzi's clip and tucked five spare magazines and two more frag grenades into his overcoat. With everything that had so far gone down, Bolan didn't want to come up short when it counted most.

Outside he retraced his steps up the alley. He reached Forty-second Street and surveyed the congestion. Traffic, both on the sidewalks and in the street, was heavy. East he saw the throngs scuttling in all directions around Times Square. Then it happened.

Bolan was looking toward Broadway when a city bus was turned into a roaring fireball, hurling wreckage and mangled bodies from the blast in all directions.

Suddenly another tremendous explosion rocked the area directly behind Bolan, a thundering double-tap that shattered his senses. Wheeling, he saw yet another bus vaporized in a cloud of whooshing fire as it rolled out of the terminal.

"I LOVE NEW YORK."

Calhoun chuckled, amused by his own words. The visual transmission from the designated member of each unit was so crystal clear, his eyes were lit by the flash of the first two explosions on the Brooklyn Bridge. In fact the destruction began to leap with such brilliance out of the bank of cameras that Calhoun felt as if he were on-site at each killzone.

From both sides of the Brooklyn Bridge, vehicles unfortunate enough to have ridden too close behind those terrorist vehicles, abandoned without warning, were swept up in the twin infernos. One fireball boiled over the bridge for inbound Manhattan traffic, while the second blast consumed several vehicles headed for Brooklyn. The steel-wire cables seemed to absorb wreckage, and skybound things Calhoun briefly recognized as bodies, like a giant sticky spiderweb. Some flaming debris sliced between the cables to plunge for the East River.

It was only the beginning. Approximately two minutes later, targeted pockets of Manhattan were quickly turned into killing zones reminding Calhoun of Beirut.

Each team with car bombs had been ordered to set off no less than one hundred pounds of either C-4 or dynamite. Some teams had grenades and lightweight sacks of C-4 to hurl. Some of the packages were on time-delayed fuses, while others were activated by remote control by a terrorist on-site—such as the one package left behind in the emergency room lobby at Bellevue Hospital.

Intent, proud of this triumphant moment, Calhoun watched the bustling doctors and nurses, the gurneys rolling in, solemn patients huddled waiting and riding out their ailments and injuries. As ordered, the minicam was attached beneath a seat in the emergency room. The scenario was almost complete, Calhoun knew. A terrorist shuffled in, checked in, sat down. Hunched over, he fixed both plastique and minicam and left. Dicey, of course, but the whole operation was a giant risk, Murphy's Law factored in for a few failures along the way. Smiling, waiting, Calhoun saw the emergency room blink out after an orange glow lit the screen for a nano-second. Bingo.

Calhoun spared a moment to enjoy the reactions of his men, and McBain. The foot-long Havana cigar nearly fell from the grizzled, sagging-jowled face of the former five-star general as he breathed, "Holy Mother of..."

Elsewhere in the command center of the Newark warehouse, six of Calhoun's finest nearly dropped the submachine guns in their hands as all eyes were riveted on the death and destruction that was not only monitored but recorded on twenty separate VCRs.

Calhoun checked his watch. The first three attacks were behind schedule, but he had factored in traffic and the Arabs' basic unfamiliarity with the city. There had been a dry run to each target, one week earlier, some scouting of each site. But Calhoun knew all he could really depend on were maps guiding each unit, recon pictures of target and vicinity and, of course, the raw hatred and determination of the fanatics to kill as many infidels in as short a time as possible.

The ex-major knew the teams had a linkup point in the city, but he didn't expect any of them to make it to the site for their final blaze of glory. And in another few minutes, once he had enough of the carnage on tape for their sponsors, they were shutting down the command center, priming it to blow up in their wake, while evacuating the States, thanks to McBain's private jet waiting at a makeshift airfield out in the Jersey countryside.

McBain cleared his throat, watching the city bus at Times Square blow up into countless metal strips and shredded body parts. Instantly the crowded sidewalks of Times Square and Broadway were turned into a stampede. Human nature took over. Civilians began to trample over one another as the terrorist unit that had set off the car bomb, plus the terrorist who had boarded the city bus only to get off and leave behind the C-4 payload, began to open up with AK-47s. As ordered, there was no audio transmission, no radio contact allowed. Each kill team was on its own. How the terrorist had managed to plant the bomb on the bus leaving Port Authority terminal, Calhoun didn't know. It wasn't part of the plan, but Calhoun had to give the guy credit for audacity and ingenuity.

Calhoun then thought he spotted distaste in McBain's eyes.

"You look like you're having some trouble with this, General."

"I never thought I'd see the day when I would be part of a plan to bring foreigner terrorists to this nation's shores to kill American citizens."

"You're not losing your stomach for what's ahead, are you, General?" Calhoun asked.

McBain scowled, puffing angrily on his stogie. "If you ask me, I always thought it should be our Ivan counterparts who needed to prove themselves to us. Not the other way around."

"They bankrolled this operation, General. Need I remind you, the cold war is dead. East has met West. We're a team now. Same goal."

"Perhaps a slightly different agenda."

"We were paid damn well, General. We knew what was ahead and what was at stake going in. We needed to show our sponsors we could train and mobilize a small army that could create mayhem and sabotage."

McBain snorted. "A small army of what? We need soldiers, not just this terrorist scum. We need disciplined, seasoned combat troops to put on the front line if we're going to pull off the big one."

"Another reason why we need this Colombian deal. I've got bona fide military men from the Colombian army who have been bought and paid for. This isn't even scratching the surface here, General. We both know there's more at stake than a billion-dollar load of cocaine and heroin."

Calhoun felt a stab of contempt for McBain. The ex-general loved money and the good life. McBain, he knew, had no one but himself to blame. Years ago the man had used his rank and position as head of Army Intelligence to sell secrets to the Russians. Later he had gathered intelligence on CIA and DEA operations in South America and sold the intel to the cartels. McBain was bought and sold, and Calhoun's sponsors had likewise presented the former Pentagon big shot with a life-or-death proposition long ago.

"Just because I'm part of it doesn't necessarily mean I have to like it, Major."

Calhoun looked back at the camera bank. One by one every camera was filled with chaos and slaughter. Another congested city street, the minicam rocking as the team leader tried to line up the kill site. Another huge explosion lifted vehicles into the air and hurtled countless scarecrow figures everywhere. Then more civilians were chopped up by a trio of converging autofire in front of Saks Fifth Avenue. Next they were dropping around Rockefeller Center, running for their lives, a good number of them stitched up the back with autofire.

A giant statue of Atlas swung into focus on another camera. It was the International Building, Calhoun knew, home to many foreign consulates, the U.S. passport office. The terrorist was mowing them down around Atlas, the visual wobbly, the terrorist obviously holding back on his AK-47's trigger. Then a fireball blew the picture out of focus. If they couldn't penetrate the lobby, they were ordered to hurl their lightweight duffel bags with payload, run like hell while firing their automatic weapons.

This was their day to shine for God.

In front of the flagpoles with the banners of 159 nations, they shined on in front of the Secretariat Building. Satchels hurled, grenades lobbed, followed by explosions. It was a vision of hell on earth. Same deal in Chinatown and Greenwich Village, garbage cans blowing and raging fire consuming pedestrians. Pan to the lobby and plaza at the Empire State Building, flaming from explosions, bodies falling in the stampede of frenzied mobs, victims taking withering bursts of lead.

"This isn't a good day for tourists," Calhoun said, and chuckled.

"We've got one down, Major. What the hell?"

Calhoun turned grim attention on the far screen, catching the alarm in Billerton's voice. The ex-major couldn't believe his eyes.

"Where is that?"

"It's the Times Square unit, sir."

Calhoun cursed. The hard face and the cold eyes of his problem from Central Park was staring right into the minicam. The big man pulled back from the minicam, and Calhoun found himself looking right into the barrel of a hand cannon. A muzzle flash, and the picture died.

Calhoun locked eyes with Billerton. He ignored McBain, who wanted to know who that guy was. Their problem was still on the loose. Whoever the unknown hitter was, Calhoun knew that unless one of the kill teams got lucky, he would see those eyes of death again.

He began to scramble for damage control, ordering the place shut down and evacuated. He would have to do some editing on that Times Square tape. No way did he want his sponsors to think he had a problem he couldn't solve.

CLEARLY THEY WERE suicide troops, and the Executioner had already begun to give Calhoun's cannon fodder all the death they could have asked for.

No sooner had the twin blasts touched off utter chaos around him than Bolan found prime targets. With the .44 Magnum Desert Eagle, Bolan had dropped three terrorists at Times Square as they shouted, "Death to infidels! Death to America!"

For at least two dozen innocent New Yorkers, it had been too little too late. While fiery wreckage was still hitting the streets and caroming off buildings, the terrorists had opened fire with their Russian assault rifles. Insane with bloodlust and driven by warped, mindless ideology of the age-old "us and them" syndrome, they had started blasting away into vehicles while terrified civilians were slaughtered where they sat, or were cut down by sweeping autofire along the sidewalks and storefronts.

Four down at the moment. How many more? How many car bombs had gone off elsewhere in the city? With the human stampedes, the police, SWAT and all law-enforcement personnel that could be marshaled to hit the streets, Bolan knew there was only so much he could do.

But he would strike down any terrorist who crossed his path. It would have to be enough. Any terrorist down and gone meant saving innocent lives.

Now Bolan was moving west on Forty-second Street. Only moments ago he had nailed another terrorist who had ignited the firestorm in front of Port Authority bus terminal. Having checked the dead Arab, Bolan had discovered the minicam mounted to the side of the enemy's head. The Executioner stared, he suspected, right at Calhoun and delivered a .44 message, obliterating the monitor. There was no sign that the terrorist was in radio communication with Calhoun, which puzzled Bolan. Calhoun wanted to watch this vision of hell on earth. Why? What purpose did Calhoun have in launching an all-out suicide attack in Manhattan?

Beyond the roaring flames to his back and front, Bolan heard the sirens, from blocks beyond, in all directions.

On the run, he hit an alley, knowing the enemy was within his grasp. He had seen the two terrorists dart into the alley moments ago. Crouched, the soldier peered around the corner. Autofire chattered and Bolan ducked back, stone chips flaying his head. He holstered the big gun and pulled out the Uzi. Return fire stopped. Bolan paused for a long moment, chanced a look and found them bolting around the corner of a building. They were heading north, into the Theater District.

The Executioner gave chase.

WITH GRIM DETERMINATION, Bolan would give back the enemy his own vision of what had been unleashed.

Uzi in hand, Bolan hugged the corner of a building where the front of the structure was smoking from flaming debris that had shot out from another apparent car bomb. Right on their heels, dogging the terrorists north of Times Square, which shrilled with horns and screams of the wounded, Bolan had witnessed the enemy duo link up with two other terrorists on the sidewalk.

Bolan heard the screaming of women and the cursing of the Arabs just ahead.

Closing on the battered opening of the building, Bolan heard, "Nahib, grab these women. We need hostages."

The door was crushed kindling as Bolan crept to the front of what appeared to be a restaurant. A woman cried out, then Bolan heard a brief stutter of weapons fire. Silence, except for sobbing.

"No one else move, or you end up like these other infidels! We will not hesitate to kill all of you!"

Bolan sucked in a deep breath. At least four enemy gunners were inside, but there could be more. If he bull-dozed his way in, there would be a panic on the enemy's part. There seemed no choice but to go in and call it on the spot. They were shock troops, hell-bent on suicide on their way to Paradise, taking as many innocent lives as they could with them.

Not on Bolan's watch.

Rising, the soldier went in low, hit the small lobby, took it all in, flank to flank and to the front. A glimpse of the carnage revealed that the terrorists had turned the restaurant into a slaughterhouse. Bodies were strewed all over the dining room, or strung out in front of the bar. Beds of glass and splintered tables littered the dining-room floor. The place reeked of cordite, smoke and blood.

Dead ahead Bolan saw a trio of faces swing his way, their eyes wild, their AK-47s rising. They had been moving on two women who were on their knees when Bolan caught them by surprise. A lightning zip of 9 mm lead waxed the trio, sent them spinning in different directions. Bolan dived behind a partition after glimpsing two more terrorists in the middle of the dining room. Autofire stitched wood above his head. Bolan scurried on, drawing the .44 Magnum Desert Eagle. If he let them gain another second, he knew it could end in a standoff that meant certain death for their intended hostages. Outside, sirens wailed.

Bolan popped up. One terrorist was snatching a woman off the floor. The guy never made his human shield in time as the soldier took off the top of his head with a thundering .44 round. The remaining terrorist had hauled in another woman, who was screaming hysterically. Just as the terrorist began to draw a bead on Bolan with his AK-47, the Executioner caressed the big handgun's trigger. Aiming low, the soldier blew the Arab's kneecap off in a cloud of blood and bone fragments.

Bolan was moving fast into the dining room as the Arab toppled, his autofire raking the ceiling. His shriek of mindless agony drowned the closing sirens.

The soldier had only a few moments to get answers. NYPD was about to storm the place. He hoped they checked their fire, because Bolan wouldn't gun down a lawman, even if he became a target.

As excruciating agony and shock seized the terrorist, the assault rifle slipped from his hand.

It appeared only three women and two men had survived the massacre.

"Go!" Bolan ordered, and put the surviving innocents out of mind as they bolted for freedom.

Looming over the terrorist, Bolan found raw hatred staring back at him. He sighted down the barrel of his gun.

"Death to infidels!" the terrorist snarled.

"Skip it. Your road to Paradise ends with me. Where can I find Calhoun? You've got two seconds."

"Stupid American swine! Your own people sold you out! We were hired by this Calhoun. He trained us for this glorious strike. He's already gone," the terrorist said through gritted teeth.

Bolan heard car doors slam. Out of the corner of his eye, the soldier saw the men in blue barrel through the door.

"Freeze!"

"I'm a Justice Department agent!"

"I don't care if you're the Pope! Drop the gun!"

Suddenly Bolan glimpsed the terrorist pulling a small pistol from his pocket. Aware death was an eye blink away from two directions, Bolan took the gamble, knowing there was no alternative. He triggered the Desert Eagle, pumping the slug into the Arab's face just as the pistol cracked, its aim thrown off by mere inches from the impact of the gruesome facial wound. Bolan felt the slug whiz past his ear.

The Executioner let the handgun fall from his grasp. He fully expected bullets to begin tearing into him, even as he repeated, "I'm a Justice Department agent!"

An eternity later, among the swirl of voices bellowing for him to get his hands up and uniformed officers converging on him, the soldier realized he would live.

For now, that was good enough. As soon as Brognola had him cut loose, Bolan would find Calhoun. One traitor had yet to know what swift justice was all about.

13

The name Ernesto Pintalbo kept popping up in Stony Man Farm's files, and whoever the man was remained a mystery to Mack Bolan. Judging from the intelligence gathered at the Farm, the name was an alias. Pintalbo's name appeared on official Miami bank documents that were tracked to numbered accounts in the Bahamas and Panama. The labyrinth of paper and money then appeared connected to a slew of fly-by-night offshore dummy companies in the Caribbean that the DEA suspected hid the real business of the latest king of the Cali cartel, one Juan Maldonado.

It was also believed that "Ernesto Pintalbo" owned this exclusive—and empty—mansion at 1542 Oceanfront Drive in North Miami Beach.

It had taken the Executioner thirty minutes to cover every room. The mansion appeared to be unoccupied. If there were cameras or listening devices inside the building, he couldn't see them. Nor could he spot motion detectors or other electronic sensors, but he couldn't discount them, either.

Now Bolan stood alone in the middle of the sprawling living room. The place was something of a monument to the bizarre and the vain, the ominous atmosphere emphasized by its seeming abandonment.

He had parked his rental car in the circular cobblestone drive near a fountain of a naked couple embracing. The sprawling grounds were ringed by lush vegetation, palm trees and ferns, with vines and ivy hanging from the coral rock wall that surrounded the estate. Strangely the wrought-iron gate had been left open. Not so strange were the security cameras tucked in vines along the top of the wall, which hadn't escaped his initial scrutiny.

Next he had come through the unlocked and mammoth, ornately carved oak double doors, armed to the teeth with his Beretta, .44 Magnum Desert Eagle and mini-Uzi in a special shoulder sling hung beneath his loose-fitting windbreaker. Attached to combat webbing were spare clips for all weapons, and one M-26 frag grenade. The Executioner was again braced for the worst possible scenario. Only this time Miami wouldn't be a repeat of Central Park.

Bolan also hadn't come alone. Right then Jack Grimaldi, Stony Man's ace pilot, was covering his back. The man had been dropped off in a cove near the estate after an earlier drive-by. Armed with an M-16 with attached M-203 grenade launcher, Grimaldi had raised Bolan moments ago, as ordered, after the soldier's thorough search of the premises. Grimaldi was hidden from the naked eye in the estate's man-made jungle, positioned in a surveillance spot to the south where he could monitor both the front and back of the mansion.

It was impossible, Bolan knew, for one man to cover the entire grounds. Since the other Stony Man warriors were off in remote parts of the world on other missions, Grimaldi had volunteered. He had often grumbled about his lack of time in the field.

The mansion and its grounds were a perfect spot for the unknown enemy to spring a trap, but the initial phase of the Miami campaign was for Bolan to be the bait.

Once reeled in, he'd gun them down, take a live one, if possible. But given the tenacity and suicidal ferocity that the enemy had so far displayed, taking a hostage for questioning was a long shot.

They were also on the enemy's home turf.

The long driveway led to the columned front of the mansion, the parking area capable of holding an armada of vehicles and hardmen. Out back were a pool, gazebo, avocado and rose gardens, then tennis courts, beyond which was docked a yacht in a private pier that looked out to the Atlantic. A strike force could creep up on the rear, unobserved until it was too late.

The Executioner checked his watch: 0902.

As he waited for the enemy to show, Bolan replayed the Manhattan nightmare in his mind. He burned with righteous anger over the lightning, suicidal and well-synchronized, if not somewhat disorganized, terrorist attacks on the city. It was only yesterday, but the insane visions of total urban warfare still clung to Bolan like a moldy shroud. Of course, he had been thwarted, but not defeated in New York. Only a few terrorists were knocked permanently out of the picture, but he figured he may have saved more than a few innocent lives.

Yesterday it had taken Brognola a lot of hard work before NYPD cut Bolan free. Both Bolan and Brognola could well understand the anger and frustration of New York officialdom. The smoke hadn't even cleared from the terrorist attacks in twenty different areas of crowded Manhattan before Bolan was whisked to JFK to board a military flight for D.C. The body count was staggering, pushing above one thousand civilian dead and wounded, and they hadn't finished sifting through the rubble and the carnage. And still Bolan had no clue as to why Calhoun had landed a foreign army of fanatics in New York and cut them loose, vicious animals who had apparently fought it out with the police, even the Army and National Guard, down to the last terrorist. With all the terrorists apparently departed in their twisted blaze of glory, Calhoun couldn't be fingered or tracked, not by legal means.

The soldier would resume the hunt in Miami.

Stony Man had compiled a list of suspected money men, couriers, middle-weight and major-league cocaine traffickers suspected of being in Maldonado's employ.

On the surface Bolan's plan, conceived at Stony Man Farm, was simple enough. It would be a search-and-destroy blitz, with Bolan and Grimaldi wrapping it up by day's end. Calhoun was most likely en route or already in Colombia to seal his business with Maldonado. It was unlikely Calhoun needed a mere three million to conclude a major drug transaction with the reigning drug king of South America. But Bolan figured Calhoun wanted Sternmann silenced after the setbacks in the Bronx and Hoboken. If Bolan and Grimaldi could create havoc for Maldonado, rupture his Florida pipeline, the drug lord might believe Calhoun was bringing him unforeseen and unwanted problems. Trouble on the U.S. mainland could flare Maldonado's natural paranoia, perhaps stall the deal long enough for Bolan to get a clear fix on the whereabouts and identities of all players concerned.

For the Miami phase, the two Stony Man warriors had flown down in a surprise package for the enemy. Until it was needed, the F-15E would be watched by a team of blacksuits from the Farm in a remote airfield near the Everglades. If the numbers fell the way Bolan intended, Maldonado's operation in southern Florida would be severely damaged. Phase two of the campaign dictated Bolan's only logical course of action was to bite off chunks of the enemy's operation, whatever and wherever it was—get them snipping at one another's heels, pointing fingers, creating dissension in the ranks.

Suddenly Grimaldi patched through on the wireless receiver in Bolan's ear. "It's show time, Sarge. Two vehicles just pulled up."

Bolan was already moving for the preselected corner in a hallway that ran past the spacious kitchen. As he pulled the Desert Eagle, he heard car doors slam out front. He moved past the doorless opening and settled in behind a statue of Atlas.

At the moment the world was, perhaps, resting on the shoulders of Bolan and Grimaldi.

"Counting seven and holding," Grimaldi told him. "Six coming through the front, our boys armed with subguns. I don't think they're here to pick up money—wait a second. You've got two more, likewise with subguns, coming around the pool. Back door men. All in all I see only one that looks like a Latin type. Rest are Anglos."

Calhoun's men. If the ex-major was present, Grimaldi would have spotted him from an intel photo. All told quite a kill team had been marshaled for Sternmann. Then again, Bolan read Sternmann as a desperate paranoid who wouldn't have come to Miami without his own backup. And whoever Ernesto Pintalbo was, it stood to reason Calhoun had done business with Maldonado in the past.

Bolan spoke into the miniature mike fixed to his webbing. "I'll take care of the back-door act, then move on the rest. You'll know when it's started. Take out the loner, then come through the front door."

"I know the drill."

"Hit and run. I want this done, quick, in and out. Good luck."

"I copy, and likewise. Over."

Bolan heard the sliding glass door open in the kitchen, then the massive front doors groaned. There was silence except for bolts cocked on automatic weapons.

"Sternmann?" an unfamiliar voice called out.

Bolan lifted the Desert Eagle and drew in a deep breath.

From the living room, the voice ordered, "Move out. Carlock, check the upstairs. Moore, shut the doors." A pause, then, "Wilkert, Marlowe, you in?"

They were coming through the opening, one after another with Uzi subguns tracking, as Bolan sighted down the barrel of the Eagle.

"We're clear."

So they thought.

The Executioner unleashed his lethal surprise. A double tap of .44 Magnum rounds from the soldier's hand cannon all but burst two crew-cut skulls, and Bolan was on the move before the corpses hit the floor.

The Executioner heard cursing and shouting. Desert Eagle holstered, Bolan primed a frag grenade, then dug out the mini-Uzi and cocked it. It didn't matter where they were; Bolan had already decided to use the place to his advantage.

On the fly, holding back on the mini-Uzi's trigger, the soldier glimpsed at least four men, fanning out, cutting loose with autofire. The startled enemy was a fraction of a second too slow in pinning the blur that was Bolan. Armed with either Uzi SMGs or the Ingram MAC-10 favored by Calhoun's killers, the hardmen cut loose with a hellstorm of 9 mm lead. Tracking bullets pockmarked the wall behind Bolan in an even line before he reached cover behind the thick base of a potted palm tree.

Bolan sprayed the living room, left to right with the mini-Uzi as two figures dashed for the bar. The soldier armed the frag grenade and let it fly. Raking the living room, forcing his adversaries to scatter and take cover wherever they could find it, Bolan saw the lethal egg land in the middle of the sunken den. He heard a curse, then someone shouted, "Grenade!"

Hosing a hardman who had nearly reached the bar, Bolan, racing away from the palm tree to try to outflank his adversaries, secured the cover of a statue of Zeus who was ringed by palmettos. Downrange the soldier's third victim cried out as the brief burst from Bolan's mini-Uzi stitched lead across the chest. Pirouetting, the hardman held back on his subgun's trigger, drilling glass all along the bar. Rounds from Bolan's stuttergun then sent the guy tumbling to the floor in a crimson splash.

The frag bomb blew. The living room, the size of a small nightclub, could contain the blast radius of fifteen yards. Seasoned combat vets, the enemy gunners were already diving, covering their heads as the detonation rocked the mansion.

Shrapnel flying around his face, Bolan hugged his own cover, after glimpsing a body riding from the smoky fireball to sail into liquor bottles. Smoke boiled, and steel fragments razored for a dangerous stretch of heartbeats. Someone screamed an obscenity, obviously in great pain.

Four down.

As Bolan calculated, the deafening frag blast momentarily shocked the surviving hardforce. Taking advantage of their fear and the brief lull in return fire, the Executioner unleathered the Desert Eagle. He then discovered he had familiar enemy company. Someone was hobbling for the cover of a palm tree near the staircase. Bolan spotted the blond gunman from Central Park. Giving the guy some lead, Bolan squeezed off a .44 round. It was only a flash of a moment, but he witnessed Calhoun's killer take the slug low in the side as blood and cloth exploded.

Two gunners poked up from the far end of the bar to unload on Bolan's position, SMGs chattering. Another gunman was blazing away from behind the railing of the staircase, winging still more bullets all over Bolan's cover, blasting plaster and glass and scything foliage.

It was no time for a standoff.

Bolan went to work to flush out the gunners from behind the bar. Concealed by stone and stump from enemy fire, as lead whined off stone and chipped off bark, Bolan slapped a fresh clip into the mini-Uzi. Lining up the sights on an aquarium, the soldier drilled a line of 9 mm slugs across the glass fronting.

Both hell and high water then overtook the bar crew. Glass rupturing, a tidal wave spewed like a maelstrom for the bar. Brilliant-colored fish flopped and spun as the wave hit the bar. If that wasn't enough to shake them up, Bolan sent .44 Magnum rounds into the mirrored ceiling over the bar. Jagged shards began to drop over the hardmen. Water pushed one gunner away from the bar, but he forged behind cover before Bolan could nail him.

From the staircase, tracking autofire had suddenly ceased snapping around Bolan.

The cavalry had arrived.

Bolan found Grimaldi, just beyond the whirl of cordite, showering glass and blown couch stuffing, holding back on his M-16's trigger. From the staircase the hardman absorbed several of Grimaldi's rounds in his chest. Fanatic to the end, the gunner bellowed in pain and rage, firing his SMG all around. His aim thrown off and dying reflexes carrying him down the steps, the hardman's wild Uzi slugs cored into the ceiling.

The Executioner bolted for the bar, mindful of the rushing water. Ahead he heard a gunman yelling in pain, cursing viciously. The gunman jumped away from the bar, and Bolan saw the reason for his sudden display of outrage.

Two piranhas had sunk razorlike teeth into the gunman's thigh. Slipping, the gunman tried to draw a bead with his Ingram on Bolan. The Executioner hurled him into the backdrop of smoke with one .44 slug through the chest.

Grimaldi, Bolan saw, was pinned behind a pillar in the foyer from steady return fire. Judging the position of autofire from the other end of the bar, Bolan hit the ceiling with a long burst from the mini-Uzi. Shards and countless glass fragments showered the enemy's position, producing an angry cry. It also halted the gunman's fire long enough for Grimaldi to pin the rising, bloodied figure to the edge of the bar with a 3-round burst of 5.56 mm bullets.

Moving out, Bolan could almost read the adrenaline burn in Grimaldi's stare as they surveyed the hellzone.

"We're clear out front," Grimaldi told Bolan. Then the Stony Man pilot moved swiftly through the smoke, padding through the water and skidding fish to check their backs.

Bolan found the blond gunner struggling to sit up. Holstering the mini-Uzi, the Executioner closed on the killer. He saw the wounded man had taken one low, most likely through the liver. Pain and shock contorted the man's face. Bolan seized the lucky moment before it ran out.

"Y-you." The enemy croaked what sounded like a chuckle. "The problem…"

Bolan kept his eyes on the wounded man as he held his hand over the blood pumping from the guy's stomach.

"The problem…Major now calls you. You're… good."

"What's your name, soldier?"

"Morrow."

"Why the attack on New York?"

"Prove it could be…done."

"Prove to who?"

"S-sponsors."

"What sponsors?"

"You may find…out…you're on the…way…try Cali…you're screwed…."

"I need answers, Morrow. In a few minutes, you're going to be dead from your wound. What my own people have learned about you and the others who were in Calhoun's Special Forces group, we know you were once decorated and honorable soldiers who fought for your country. Talk to me, clean yourself. Help me restore some honor to you and the others."

"Skip the patriotic speech. Started in Laos…Gulf War sucked…high-tech bull…Calhoun made some serious buddies…America…whole world…change is coming…you…nobody…can stop it."

Bolan knew the moment was slipping away fast. "Stop what?"

"Paradise…a new earth…after the ashes…like a Phoenix rising…new human race…"

"Is Calhoun right now in Colombia to nail his deal with Maldonado?"

Morrow gritted his teeth, the whites of his eyes showing. "Drug deal...only small part...final shipment...can't stop Calhoun...sponsors. Biggest load ever... Man, we had a lot...of good times...R and R in this place...I'll...miss Miami...."

Bolan had a day's worth of questions to fire off, but he knew Morrow was out of time.

"Who is Ernesto Pintalbo, soldier?"

Morrow coughed, laughed. "Big...brass...Bill..."

Bolan's gaze narrowed, dark instinct flaring, as he suspected the answer before he heard it. "Bill who?"

"The...general...Mc—"

Morrow toppled over in a bed of glass, lifeless eyes staring back at Bolan.

So McBain was Ernesto Pintalbo. How deep he was connected and how long or why to Maldonado and the Cali cartel, Bolan didn't know. But the Executioner was yanking tickets with no refunds from there on out. Long ago McBain had turned on his duty and his country. That much was clear, and Bolan was rolling on to Colombia to give out what was deserved. The dead in New York, he suspected, were only the start of whatever was on Calhoun's plate.

Frustrated, Bolan looked at the dead man for a moment, then turned and found Grimaldi coming from the bar. There was a grim bewilderment in Grimaldi's eyes Bolan had never seen.

After surveying the carnage, Grimaldi looked from Morrow to Bolan. "These guys all had sterling military records. They were the best of the best. Now they're training terrorist armies to kill Americans and moving drugs to parts unknown with a final goal we don't have a clue about, talking about a new earth after the ashes. Sarge, what in hell are we dealing with?''

Bolan could only stare back at his friend, wishing he had at least one solid answer.

AZTEC INTERNATIONAL occupied the top floor of a newly constructed office building in downtown Miami. In fact the entire building belonged to Juan Maldonado. Mack Bolan was only interested in a lawyer named Armando Castilina at the moment.

Armed with only his Beretta beneath his windbreaker and a large manila envelope, Bolan moved into the reception area of the suite. It featured much the same decor of oil paintings of South American landscapes and Indian warriors, palm trees and mirrored walls and ceiling Bolan had left behind in Miami Beach. Beyond the windows of the suite, the lawyer had a sweeping view of the gleaming white skyline of Miami Beach across Biscayne Bay.

Bolan wasn't there for the view or the sunshine. Stony Man Farm, with Brognola working his contacts with the DEA, had pinned Castilina as the front man for the Maldonado organization in Miami. Here they masked their real agenda with endeavors in computers, powerboat and small-aircraft design and building and, of course, real estate and banking. Juan Maldonado was quite the entrepreneur.

His days in Miami were numbered. Bolan had the file, ready to deliver to Castilina. Brognola's DEA contacts had laid the groundwork, and it was up to Bolan and Grimaldi to finish the grim business in Miami. If the Executioner and Grimaldi succeeded in what they planned, it would be the most crushing and daring blow ever landed against any major drug organization.

When the pretty, dark-haired Hispanic receptionist looked up, Bolan said, "I have an appointment to see Mr. Castilina."

Suspicious, she asked, "Your name, sir?"

Bolan showed her a wry smile. "My name is Mr. Problem. I'm not on his appointment book, so don't bother to check."

He moved for the double mahogany doors with the embossed nameplate as the receptionist got on the intercom, rattling off rapid-fire Spanish to her boss. Bolan went through the door, saw his puppet for the final drama in Miami rising from behind his desk.

The intel photos of Castilina from the Farm did the lawyer justice in person. The lawyer was lean, handsome, black hair gelled back to a ponytail, dark eyes full of pride and arrogance that he could successfully do his master's work and reap the benefits of the good life. The Armani suit and diamond-studded Rolex watch were a little much if he was looking for low-profile, but Bolan had never met a narcotics trafficker who didn't like to flash, at least a little, keep the ladies cooing and the cronies envious.

Substance always beat style, even on a bad day. Make no mistake, the lawyer was still a drug dealer, all flash, little in the way of character or muscle to back up the mouth and the front. He was perfect for Bolan's plan.

Castilina's typical brazen display fit the total picture of men who moved above the law, dirtied, but used some of the law to keep their hands clean. Lawyers, judges, policemen were on the payroll, and everyone could be bought for a price, anything in advanced technology for sale. Maldonado, like his predecessors in the Cali cartel, moved these days with sophisticated high-tech equipment to invent and secure newer and safer routes for cocaine and heroin into the States. Times had changed some, with major drug lords stepping up into the high-tech age to stay one step ahead, but they still ruled through fear, intimidation, bribery and violence.

"What is the meaning of this? Who are you?" Castilina raged.

Bolan closed the door behind him. With a look around the ostentatious office with its wet bar, Jacuzzi whirlpool, massive conference table, giant-screen TV, Bolan found they were alone. If trouble arose, Bolan had Grimaldi waiting in the downstairs garage, raised by radio, if necessary. But a shoot-out in broad daylight in the middle of downtown Miami with any goons acting as security would seriously hamper Bolan's agenda. No, he was there to present Armando Castilina with a proposition.

"I'm here on behalf of Señor Maldonado," Bolan said. "It would greatly help your cause if you listened carefully to me—and don't buzz for security."

"I do not know you. You are sent from Señor Maldonado?"

"In a roundabout way."

"What is your name?"

"Let's just call me Mr. Problem."

"I do not find this game amusing, 'Señor Problema.'"

"I didn't come here for laughs. And this is no game."

Castilina froze, staring at Bolan. He had to have figured that some problem, indeed, had stepped forth in his world of paranoia and shadow moves. The hand came up from under his desk. The receptionist barged in, but Castilina, throwing up a restraining hand, said, "It's all right, Conchita. Please, close the door. I am not to be disturbed."

When they were alone again, Bolan moved for the desk, dropped the file in front of the lawyer.

"What is that?"

"It's a list of your people I need to deliver a message to," Bolan said. "Open it."

The lawyer snickered, but sized Bolan up with mounting anxiety. "Who are you?"

"If you or the others I wish to have a conference with are worried about getting busted, I assure you I'm not legal heat."

Staring at Bolan, the lawyer opened the envelope and removed the computer printout.

"I want you to call every man on that list," Bolan said, and drew a look of anger from Castilina. "Aztec International owns an industrial complex here in Miami. You build boats and planes there, remember? I want those men to be at the main hangar," Bolan said, checking his watch, "in three hours."

"You're crazy. These are respectable businessmen. They have appointments, schedules, hectic days...."

"Fit me in."

"I cannot just call them and order them at your whim to be where you want them to be when you want them. What is this about?"

Bolan put ice in his voice. "If you don't bring those men together, where and when I want them, I'll come back here and give you a problem you won't be able to handle. What's more, if you fail to contact these men and don't bring them where I ask when I ask, I'll be unable to stop them, and you, from being arrested."

Castilina hesitated. "Arrested? For what?"

"Don't jack me around. We both know the truth. I'm prepared to keep you and those men on the list from being arrested, tried and convicted and incarcerated for the rest of your lives for narcotics trafficking, money laundering, conspiracy—name it. If you fail me, this could get back to Señor Maldonado. Fail me, you fail him. Are we clear?''

Some confidence returned to Castilina's eyes. "First of all, we do not 'build' boats or planes at our complex. We merely ship parts, store—''

"Whatever. Are you going to do what I want in the interest of Señor Maldonado? Do you want to call him? Describe me? When I'm sent to you to help you help him? Do you want to upset his busy day when he depends on you to keep things running smooth?''

"Okay, okay.'' Nodding, Castilina looked as if he were a believer. "You say—and I'm not admitting guilt of any wrongdoing—these men are about to be arrested?''

"I have a way to help them out. If I help them, it helps you, and you in turn have helped Mr. Maldonado. I can save you from future trouble from the law.''

"How?''

"Just be there.''

Castilina tapped his chin with forefinger. "I will do my best to gather these men.''

"Your best better be good enough. I assume you have a car phone. I'll need the number.''

Scowling, Castilina jotted down the number and handed the slip of paper to Bolan.

"When you're all there, I'll call you. One other thing. I want all nonessential personnel in and around the main hangar cleared out. We'll need complete privacy. Can you manage that?''

"Yes. And, I will warn you, Mr. Whoever-you-are, this had better be something of great importance.''

"I assure you,'' Bolan said, and threw the Cali cartel's

front man in South Florida a graveyard smile, "if you don't want law trouble in the future, you won't want to miss this opportunity."

"A matter of life or death, is that it?"

Bolan returned the lawyer's skepticism with a departing hard eye, and said, "You could most definitely say that."

THE SNOW JOB WORKED, but the Executioner had known going in that Castilina's natural paranoia would get the best of him.

An armada of limos and other luxury vehicles was parked near the giant main hangar. Through his field glasses, stretched out in a prone position on a knoll roughly two hundred yards north of the gathering enemy, Bolan watched. Doors opened to disgorge dozens of men in stylish suits and dark shades. Bulges showed beneath the suit jackets, windbreakers, a couple of hardmen even brazenly displaying hardware shoulder holstered over aloha shirts. They were looking all around, mouths working overtime, angry expressions directed at Castilina, who was gesturing and looked to be giving at best, Bolan assumed, lame excuses to quell their indignation.

As instructed, the workforce inside the main hangar was being cleared out. The hangar was big enough to hold three, maybe four 747s, but all Bolan spotted beyond the open doors were private jets. A few limos rolled into the hangar. More grim-faced men piled out of vehicles. Bolan only knew them by name and their dark reputations via Stony Man intel. It was quite a flock of human vultures: front men, dealers, couriers, lawyers, bankers, accountants, hardmen who manned the cutting labs and distribution chains, moving product north and west out of Florida. Who said Miami was no longer king of cocaine? Bolan thought.

With his handheld radio, Bolan patched through to Grimaldi. "Striker to Fire Eagle, come in, Fire Eagle."

"Fire Eagle here and ready for takeoff."

"It's show time, Fire Eagle. Our flock has gathered. Hustle up. You copy, Fire Eagle?"

"I'm rolling now, Striker. Once I'm airborne, ETA is approximately three minutes. See you after the fireworks. Over and out."

Three minutes could be an eternity, Bolan knew. Down there he saw them getting more antsy, shuffling around, moving inside the hangar, men gesticulating, all bent out of shape.

According to the DEA, Aztec International had purchased this land near the Dolphin Expressway less than two years earlier. In that short time, Maldonado and his so-called business associates had erected hangars for a fleet of private jets, twin-engine planes, powerboats. There were tractor trailers, sleek jets and twin-engine planes parked haphazardly around another half-dozen hangars, or near the runway. Workers were now milling around near a group of trailers, far to the south, well clear of what would soon be ground zero.

Bolan spotted Castilina outside the hangar. Grimaldi would get one good strafe before they figured out they'd been duped. Any runners who took the long dirt road from the complex for the expressway would be cut off by Bolan.

The Executioner checked his watch. The two-seater F-15E was outfitted with two Pratt & Whitney turbofan engines capable of kicking twenty-four thousand pounds of thrust into the fighter jet Grimaldi had code-named

Fire Eagle. Bolan knew the ace pilot could max out at 2.5 Mach and be there shortly once he was airborne.

Fire Eagle also carried twelve tons of high explosive death. Four Sparrow missiles, four heat-seeking Sidewinders and an M-61 Vulcan cannon, capable of blazing out 6,000 rounds per minute, made it the premier fighter jet in the world. Bolan knew Fire Eagle needed only a fraction of that payload to make Miami a wrap. Aerial recon photos of the target complex, and the computer-simulated dry run from takeoff to the main hangar at Stony Man Farm, should be all the ace pilot needed to deliver the fatal blow.

Prep work done, school was out and the real thing was about to shatter the world of Juan Maldonado.

If a DEA informant deep inside Aztec International was right, four to five tons of cocaine alone was stored in plane parts in the main hangar, supposedly ready for distribution within the next few days.

To some extent what Bolan had told Castilina was true. The DEA was prepared to raid the hangar and move on other Maldonado front operations in the Miami area. Of course, the Executioner had bluffed the man and his trafficking legion into taking the bait that was the prelude to their own demise. Before they realized what was happening, it would be too late.

Raising Grimaldi one last time before the finale, Bolan was told one minute and counting by the ace pilot.

Bolan quickly dialed Castilina. The familiar angry voice snarled back, "Yes. Where are you? We are all here waiting for your great announcement!"

The Executioner was moving fast for his rental car. He had lost sight of Castilina. For some reason a few of the crews were piling back into their vehicles. Background noise in the transmission revealed a babble of furious voices speaking a mix of Spanish and English.

West, Bolan spotted the fighter bird swooping in for the kill, closing fast to target, maybe two miles out.

"I'm close," Bolan said.

"Now what? These men don't have all day!"

"I have a message for you, Castilina."

Bolan saw the first of two Sidewinders flaming away from the wings of Fire Eagle.

"What?" Castilina barked.

"Crime doesn't pay."

Before he severed the connection, Bolan heard them cursing and shouting, "We're being attacked!"

They were pointing at the streaking warbird, or running for their lives, scattering in all directions, jumping into vehicles when the missiles plunged, dead center into the hangar. A blinding flash and a roaring fireball vaporized the structure. For added measure, Grimaldi strafed a few fleeing vehicles with M-61 Vulcan fire before sweeping past the target. A thundering line of HE 20 mm shells nearly put the finishing touches on the total destruction.

There were a few runners who had gotten the jump before ground zero erupted.

Bolan was revving the engine, hitting the dirt road to cut off one vehicle that barely escaped the consuming firecloud. Another vehicle had been lifted by the blast and hurled into the side of a warehouse to land on its side.

Out of the corners of his eyes, Bolan saw Fire Eagle soar past the mushrooming cloud. The F-15E climbed rapidly, a silver streak rolling against the gleaming white skyline of Miami, to head back to base.

It was Bolan's show now.

He reached the end of the dirt road and grabbed the M-16 with attached M-203 grenade launcher. A vehicle, wreckage slamming the earth behind it, was racing for escape. Bolan was out of the car, lining up the M-203. He gave the target some lead and caressed the trigger. Downrange the 40 mm grenade hit the limo on its nose, lifting its shattered hull into the air on a smoking thunderclap.

A bloodied figure crawled from the crushed hull of the limo perched against the warehouse.

"Y-you bastard!"

Slowly Bolan walked toward Castilina. The Executioner lifted the M-16 as the lawyer staggered to his feet.

"You gave me your word!"

The guy was digging into his shredded suit jacket. "Bastard! You said we would not be harmed!"

The lawyer was clawing out a small pistol, then teetered as he fumbled to keep a firm grip on the weapon.

"Wrong," Bolan said. "I promised to save you from future legal trouble."

The Executioner squeezed the M-16's trigger and sealed his oath to Castilina.

14

The problem had more than likely struck again. Forget no call from Miami—Morrow never missed a scheduled check-in. Hell, Calhoun was no sooner situated in McBain's Cartagena villa than the call from Cali had sounded a new and desperate alarm. Razor-sharp sixth sense warned him the worst had happened in Miami. With paranoia working double time, within and all around him, Calhoun feared another agenda of serious trouble was on an already overflowing plate.

The problem had either landed in Colombia or was en route.

South America's latest and deadliest drug lord hadn't come right out and said he had taken a devastating blow on the U.S. mainland, but the words and the threatening tone were clear enough.

"There has been a major problem that I have suffered to the north. If I suffer, others suffer. You and I and the others will talk in person very soon. As we speak, I am sending my people to find out just what the fuck is going on with you."

Maldonado had called an hour ago, and the words still rang in Calhoun's ears like a death knell.

Hands on the railing of the wooden balcony, Calhoun stared out over the Spanish colonial fortress city along the Caribbean. In the distance lights burned from the old buildings, the scattering of churches, with the fortresses tucked, here and there, among the thick walls and moats. It was well into the night, and the sounds of Spanish and Caribbean music drifted up from Cartagena proper, carried to his ears on a cool sea breeze. Civilians were having a gay old time down there.

While he was faced with a potential fiasco, once again. Without Sternmann's three million dollars, Calhoun would have to go and barter for it from the only man—besides the problem—he had ever feared.

The Russians were in the upstairs suite. For twenty minutes now they had been reviewing the spliced and edited tape of the Manhattan siege. Looking over his shoulder, he saw the ex-KGB assassin nod. Kuschka grinned over a bouncing shot capturing the Staten Island ferry turned to a listing fireball. Warheads from two RPG-7s had scored hits, one having struck the upper tier, while the other missile scored a direct hit on the hull. Then the Times Square attack, all of ten seconds, the problem edited out, of course. A scene on a subway platform, Wall Street, commuters blown all over the platform and to the tracks by autofire. The ghoulish smile came back, about as close a reaction to approval as Calhoun knew he would see on Kuschka.

He had know the killer for almost thirty years. He wasn't even certain if Kuschka was currently in-service or former KGB. Not that it mattered.

Their journey to the present had begun in Laos and Cambodia, where they both decided it was better to kill for profit than simply kill. Years later, working for the CIA in Afghanistan, he had met Kuschka again.

A shipment of nerve gas, which Calhoun had stolen from Palestinian terrorists in the Bekaa Valley, had finally been sold to Kuschka, the highest bidder. Kuschka, in turn, had used the nerve gas to wipe more than a few Afghan villages off the map where the Hinds and soldiers and Spetsnaz commandos couldn't get to without suffering severe casualties at the hands of ferocious mujahideen guerrillas.

Long story, ancient history, Calhoun thought, just like all the pirates who ever tramped through Cartagena, or Francis Drake putting the torch to homes and churches, while looting the city in the name of the queen.

Maybe it was high time, Calhoun decided, to act on some real cutthroat instincts, do some looting himself. The deal with Maldonado would go through, one way or another. A six-hundred-million-dollar load was on the line, more than a billion at stake on the receiving end once the product was cut in European labs or at the hands of the Russian Mafia. It could turn out here in Colombia the power of the gun had to exceed the power of money. He judged Maldonado's people as vicious and treacherous, standard fare for their ilk, but they were no match for seasoned combat vets who knew how to kick ass and take names in the blink of an eye.

Calhoun watched the focus of his anger disgorge from luxury vehicles below. Maldonado's entourage of grim-faced men with angry eyes and distinctive bulges beneath their jackets strode for the front door. One last sweep of the blackness surrounding the grounds, and Calhoun found three of his own men, armed with Heckler & Koch MP-5 subguns, patrolling the perimeter. He didn't like that there was no gate around the premises, no cameras, electronic sensors, not even guard dogs. There were only palm trees, a man-made lagoon, other vegetation to discourage unwelcome visitors. Anybody could just walk right onto the grounds. But McBain explained this was his vacation home, where he entertained ladies and VIPs. He hired security when necessary. Was the man a fool? So bloated by money and pleasure, so well connected by his intel handouts to the criminal elite, living on past glory and favors in Colombia he thought he didn't need to cover his back?

To the west, two Bell JetRangers were grounded on the helipad, fueled and ready to go. Just in case it hit the fan.

Bewildered and worried, Calhoun moved into the suite. He folded his arms behind his back, giving full view to all present the holstered Beretta 92-Fs, butts out for a cross-draw. If there was a problem with the Colombians, he would take care of matters personally, just like in Central Park. He—"they"—needed this deal nailed, done and gone.

The scar-faced ex-KGB assassin snapped off the video with his remote. "Impressive, Comrades, very impressive."

Perched on a stool at the bar, brandy snifter in hand, McBain grumbled around his cigar. "Was there ever any doubt, 'Comrade'?"

Kuschka rose from his chair, smiling. On the divan three men in black leather jackets who had been introduced as Boris, Igor and Gregor but who hadn't said one word in the past hour, stared at McBain.

Calhoun had four of his best present. Elbows on the bartop, Billerton scanned the room with a narrowed gaze. A .44 AutoMag was leathered in Billerton's shoulder holster. Beneath the bar Calhoun knew a SPAS-12 autoshotgun was within easy reach for Billerton. Scattered around the Spartanly furnished room, Augustly, Cuckowe and Surgeons monitored the meet in grim silence, smoking, .44 AutoMags in plain sight.

"No doubt, at all, General. I merely needed to find out just how serious and dedicated you are."

"So we passed the test for the motherland," McBain growled, blowing smoke. "Sure Stalin just grew a woody in his grave."

"A what?" Kuschka asked.

"Forget it," McBain said. "If you ask me, that whole business in Manhattan was unnecessary. Since then we've had nothing but problems. Any word from Miami, Major?"

"No," Calhoun answered.

"Great. More problems. Now our Colombian friends are here for the rest of their money, which we don't have."

Kuschka held up a hand. "The money problem has been taken care of as of this afternoon."

"What about the three million for our other merchandise?" Calhoun asked.

"The soldiers we wanted? It is—how do you Americans say?—a done deal. I must congratulate you. You did a splendid job, recruiting, training and fielding a small army that proved it would fight to the death, if properly motivated. However, Comrades, we knew they were suicidal fanatics before this venture. In the future we will be training and fielding soldiers of the highest caliber. Mere fanaticism may not prove enough. We will discuss this later, once we conclude this business and are safely on our way."

They were coming up the stairs. Calhoun watched as Ricardo Ochoba, Maldonado's right hand, rolled into the room, all arrogance and obvious anger and indignation. The swarthy, dark-haired Ochoba was all five feet six inches tall, and 140 pounds, but his reputation was well-known and feared throughout Colombia and beyond. An orphaned punk and a thief when he was a kid, he was rumored to have been one of the first but most efficient assassins for the notorious Medellín cartel before Pablo Escobar was killed. While killing for Escobar, he had moved up the pecking order with each vicious murder of a politician, informant, even a DEA agent on occasion. Ochoba had, of course, moved on to greener pastures since, teaching himself how to handle everything from small aircraft to accounting books, supercomputers and sophisticated technology that had become a staple for the new drug regime.

Four large, long-haired goons stood at parade rest behind Ochoba.

"Comrade Ochoba," Kuschka greeted, "it is good to see you again."

"I wish," Ochoba said, running an angry gaze around the room, "I could say the same. I will get right to business. Señor Maldonado is extremely unhappy with recent events."

Calhoun felt the little man's dark stare boring into him. He was ready for it to turn ugly.

"Señor Maldonado wishes to know why one of our most important people in New York is dead, along with his security detail in an apparent and mysterious shootout in Central Park. He wants to know why, according to first reports, one lone man walked into our main office in Miami and forced a strange gathering of nearly all of our most important and influential personnel. Then why they were blown up, halfway across Biscayne Bay, along with twenty million dollars' worth of product stored at the spot where these men died. We are only gathering first reports, but everything we have heard so far reeks of trouble. To sum it up, are we in danger of any kind?"

Now Calhoun felt eyes flickering his way. He felt his

heart skip a beat. Sure enough, the problem had kicked Maldonado right in the teeth. Morrow and the others he'd sent to pick up Sternmann's money were dead. It seemed the problem had likewise gotten to Sternmann. Even as he felt the blood pressure pulsing in his temples, Calhoun maintained a poker face.

"We were hit in Central Park. It was a meet between myself and Santiago," Calhoun said, "to iron out some details. Sorry you lost your man, but it was unavoidable. Who the hitter was, I couldn't say, but he's been taken care of."

"You're sorry! Unavoidable! He's been taken care of! We suspect whoever caused you a problem in New York somehow followed your people to Miami. First our man in New York is dead, killed by an assailant or an opposing unknown force, and you, we fear, may have brought us all unwanted trouble."

"That hasn't been proved."

"Not proved?"

"The rest of the funds were wired into your account this morning," Kuschka injected. Money talk seemed to calm Ochoba. "We can conclude this business and be on our way as soon as you wish. If there was a problem, and the major says it was taken care of, then I must believe it is as he says."

"Indeed," Ochoba said. "Unfortunately for all concerned, things are no longer so simple."

"Wait a second," McBain growled. "What are you saying? A few setbacks, we've paid up and now you don't want the deal? Is that what I'm hearing? I've put five million of my own money into this deal."

"Not necessarily, General."

Calhoun clenched his jaw. "Then what, 'necessarily'?"

"The price has gone up. Señor Maldonado has suffered his own setbacks."

"How much?" Calhoun rasped.

"For the setback, his time and trouble and aggravation, his loss of the diplomat courier for our product, the mysterious destruction of our operation in Miami that will take months, perhaps years to rebuild, his loss of sleep, general anxiety and just distrust and anger, an additional ten million must be wired into the account by no later than noon tomorrow."

"Or the deal's off?" McBain said, looking as if he would bite his cigar in two. "So you're making us accountable for your problems?"

"Only if our problems appear connected to your problems. General," Ochoba said, moderating his tone, "you and Señor Maldonado have a history, have up to now had a good working relationship. He is indebted to you for information passed on over the years about DEA and CIA operations in our country. He feels the debt has long since been repaid, with this villa, with generous rewards of money. The rest of you, he has only met once before. It has proved a mutually rewarding partnership—up to now. Depending on what happens, this may be the third and final transaction."

"It's the biggest one yet, and we need to move quickly," Calhoun said. "We want this deal as bad as you."

"Perhaps. It is not so simple. Most of the product is now secured and ready to go."

"Most? Wait a second," Calhoun said, "are you telling us what we've paid for is not all there?"

"Yes and no. There are problems with unforeseen opposition."

"The DEA?" Calhoun asked.

"Yes. Among other problems. Señor Maldonado will speak to all of you soon. General, I see your helicopters outside. I assume your pilots can safely and quickly fly yourself and the others to Señor Maldonado's estate near Cali?"

McBain, glowering at Calhoun, said, "When do we fly? I'm anxious to conclude this. I've invested too much in this deal to watch it blow up in my face."

"He will expect you right away. Give me two hours to return to my office here, make the call and the arrangements. Be ready to go at a moment's notice. When you meet with him, he will explain."

Without another word, Ochoba and his crew left.

When they were alone, Calhoun felt Kuschka's cold, penetrating stare.

"Comrade, is there something I need to know about?"

"There's no problem," Calhoun told the ex-KGB assassin.

"Everything is under control?"

"It is."

As soon as he heard the words leave his mouth, Calhoun knew it was a lie.

"WHAT HAS HAPPENED to this once beautiful land of emeralds and coffee?"

"It isn't the land, it's the people and the changing times brung about by the new El Dorado."

"The myth is true?"

"All that glitters is not gold."

Twenty minutes ago Bolan had finished saying the other half of the password to his DEA contact in Cartagena, arrangements once again shored up by Hal Brognola. The short, thick-set, mustachioed man called Carlos had since given Bolan the information he needed to pick up the hunt for Calhoun.

They stood on the shore of the lagoon, its still, dark waters reflecting light glowing from the stone relic of Fort San Felipe de Barajas.

Grimaldi was waiting in a Land Rover on a nearby rise overlooking the lagoon. Even before they had left Stony Man Farm for Miami, Brognola had gotten busy, laying the groundwork for their mission in Colombia. A team of blacksuits now secured the F-15E on a remote Caribbean island near Cartagena. From there, Bolan and Grimaldi had flown to a joint DEA–Special Forces outpost, near the Magdalena River, roughly three hundred miles south of the fortress city. They hadn't exactly received VIP treatment from Colonel Willow, commanding officer of the outpost. Willow had his orders that Special Agents Belasko and Griswald were to be given carte blanche—transportation, weapons, anything they needed.

"You are now up to speed, Mr. Belasko."

Bolan stared at Carlos, read the dark confusion in his eyes. Beyond his own mission, the soldier had decisions to make.

"The man you seek is right now at McBain's villa. A little over an hour ago, they flew in by helicopter. I will call off my surveillance, as you request. We now know, at least, Maldonado's men are meeting with McBain and Calhoun, as my source learned earlier. For years my informants wondered why Maldonado climbed to the top of the heap so quickly. He was always one step ahead of the DEA and the CIA. He has bought out many people, just like his predecessors, or killed them or had them killed. 'Silver or lead,' that is the saying in Colombia among the traffickers. In this country and in

America, it seems money can buy the souls of many. Yes, a CIA informant I work with knows of Calhoun and McBain. They have been in Colombia before, in the company of Maldonado. It is believed several large shipments of the precursor chemicals for cocaine—ether, acetone, kerosene—are brought here from Germany, it would seem stored in industrial machinery from this Max Tielig you mentioned earlier."

"I hope your informants are right," Bolan said. "There's no room for failure on this."

"Are Colombia and its evil of drugs familiar to you?"

"I've passed this way before."

"Then surely you know that the big busts and seizures and captures of narcotics traffickers are successful mostly because of informants. These men have not failed me yet."

"You said three DEA agents are missing?"

"Bad news travels to me at lightning speed. I heard about Maldonado's misfortunes in Miami. I know a diplomat long suspected of smuggling perhaps untold hundreds of kilos into the United States via diplomatic pouch was killed in Central Park. I'm sure Maldonado is aware of this also. Yes, I had three agents, deep inside the Maldonado organization, turn up missing for a scheduled rendezvous with a man I have in Cali. You know that Colonel Willow is prepared to move on a major processing lab in the jungle at dawn, and perhaps even Maldonado knows this. If Maldonado is true to form, he has taken my people to this lab. He has done this sort of thing before. He uses human shields in the face of potential violence while he washes his hands of blood with bribery and corruption all over this country. Someone he thinks will speak out against him...well, none has so far succeeded."

"Standard operating procedure for Maldonado's kind. It's unfortunate."

"Yes. These drug lords and their organizations, the poison and the misery they spread. Countless suffer, live in poverty, go into debt, kill themselves or others, sell all pride and dignity of their families for this evil. And these men have more money, resources, even counter-intelligence these days than we have at our disposal. They are like cockroaches. Step on one, once the light is turned off more skitter out of the cracks. It is a never ending battle, but to quit means to let bad men devour all of us."

"It's why I'm here," Bolan said. "I know all about plans coming apart, but I intend to help the colonel out."

"By leading the raid?"

"Cut off the sources, you end the problem. Right now my source is waiting for me in a villa a few miles away. If those men are being held captive as human shields, or if the worst has happened to them, after the cooperation Colonel Willow has given myself and my partner, I don't think I could just walk away in good conscience without having a part in the colonel's raid."

"And it may help further your own agenda?"

"I have no agenda other than seeing the men I'm after go down and stay down, to save innocent lives where I can and to see a few good men go on breathing to carry on the good fight."

Carlos nodded. "Tell me—were you in New York or Miami recently? Never mind," he quickly added. "I wonder who you really are. I am beginning to think Colombia will never again be the same once you leave."

The Executioner hustled to the waiting Land Rover. If Carlos was right, it should be an easy penetration of the enemy grounds.

But getting in was the easiest part.

15

The lone sentry at the stone archway appeared suspicious. When he began to look toward the first of two dark shadows rolling out of the brush, the sound-suppressed Beretta chugged in Bolan's fist. One whispering 9 mm Parabellum round between the eyes dropped the guard where he stood, his MP-5 subgun hitting the ground beside his body without an involuntary warning shot going off.

Perhaps Calhoun's man had caught the distant rumble of the Land Rover's engine before Grimaldi parked the vehicle inside a thicket at the base of a deep slope. From roughly one hundred yards away from the villa on the hill, the two-man shock force, their faces and hands blackened with combat cosmetics, had made a swift and silent run for the target.

One down. But how many more enemy guns? And had they actually made the target site unobserved? Bolan glimpsed the handheld radio on the sentry's belt and knew it was possible the dead gunner could have reported in a potential problem.

Combat senses on adrenaline overdrive, they moved on.

Both warriors toted M-16s with M-203 grenade launchers attached under the barrels. Their webbing was fitted with garrotes, frag grenades, spare clips for assault rifles and side arms. Bolan didn't intend to take prisoners. Whatever was beyond the villa in Colombia, he would deal with Maldonado in short order. It helped their cause somewhat that the villa was isolated from the city, the only apparent residence on gently rolling hill country. Of course, the last thing they needed was a confrontation with Colombian authorities, who were notorious for corruption and graft and would most likely prove indifferent to their "official status" as special agents of the United States Justice Department.

Bolan had come too far to let anything or anyone on either side of the law stop him now.

The Executioner wanted Calhoun's head, and knew he was within striking distance.

Before moving on the target, Bolan had surveyed the Spanish-style villa and grounds through infrared binoculars. Two sleek executive-type choppers were grounded. They would have to go, for there would be no hasty fighting evacuation for the enemy. Panning on, he had marked Calhoun, standing on the balcony. It was his first sighting of the traitorous ex-SF major since it began on the killing grounds of Long Island. Intel photos nailed Calhoun, the man older than his service years, of course. But there was no mistaking the one savage Bolan needed to take down if he was going to flush out and deliver the killing blow to whomever Calhoun was working for, perhaps even begin to unravel the mystery of Hydra. And Bolan had spotted another player. Calhoun was embroiled in an argument with a tall man Bolan couldn't identify from prior intelligence. He hoped they were still locked in angry words up there.

It wouldn't be long now.

Grimaldi, M-16 poised, took the west side of the driveway. So far—other than his neglect at mentioning the choppers—Carlos's intel was on the money. There appeared to be fewer ferns, palms, brush along the sides of the driveway than anywhere else around the grounds. Swift and quiet, the two men made speedy progress toward their final destination. Light from the villa grounds, the city, the stars and the moon, enabled Bolan and Grimaldi to move on without night-vision goggles. Cautious, they forged on, paralleling each other through lush vegetation, skirting around thick brush where openings led to narrow paths. They kept their eyes peeled for booby traps.

From his earlier surveillance, Bolan figured the driveway was about fifty yards long before it hit the front of the villa.

Closing hard, the doomsday numbers were tumbling.

And it went to hell two seconds later.

Through a break in the vegetation, Bolan caught brief sight of the mystery guest on the balcony giving the perimeter a sudden hard search. Sensing unseen danger, Bolan crouched behind a palm tree. He looked over at Grimaldi and waved him down.

Two armed shadows were walking down the driveway, seeming to have rolled their way out of nowhere. As if they sensed Bolan was almost on top of them, they looked his way. Up to that point, the Executioner had still hoped to gain some edge of surprise with silent death. He still went for the quiet kill.

It proved a near deadly error in judgment for Bolan.

Although Calhoun's men had turned their backs on honor, duty and loyalty to their country, these men were still seasoned combat veterans. The slightest sound, an intuitive sense that an enemy was hunting them, had triggered the silent alarms in their heads. Not giving them the chance to act on their instincts, Bolan stroked the Beretta's trigger twice, giving the enemy a double tap of death when another shadow to his far left flank opened up with autofire.

Catching the sudden movement, Bolan darted ahead, M-16 coming off his shoulder. The barrage of enemy fire chopped up brush behind the soldier. Firing from the hip, Bolan winged the gunman with a lucky burst from his M-16. SMG flaming in the hardman's fists, the guy tried to stay on his feet, but Bolan held back on his assault rifle's trigger and the shadow landed in thick brush in a boneless sprawl. Leathering the Beretta, Bolan surged on.

Chaos seized the villa and its grounds.

A loud whine of turbo engines snared Bolan's attention. To the west he saw the two sleek choppers lifting off. Along the front porch, and from the upstairs balcony, at least a half-dozen hardmen were taking up positions. Enemy subguns ripped loose in synch, two from the balcony, four more from behind the columned front porch.

Bolan and Grimaldi were forced to ground as bullets ripped up the soft earth or drilled tree bark. Covered behind a thick palmetto, the Executioner checked his friend and found the ace pilot had likewise secured the cover of a palm tree.

Sporadic gunfire followed after a few long heartbeats.

The soldier saw the choppers hugging the grounds, vanishing beside the villa. They were going for flight, out back.

Bolan braved the lull, peering around the base of the tree. Gunmen were scattering away from the front porch. He gestured he'd take the balcony, and Grimaldi the porch. On cue the two men wheeled, low around their cover, and triggered their M-203s. Downrange the twin blasts shattered the enemy on the balcony and porch. Bodies cartwheeled on the smoky fireballs, a torn figure skidding over the roof of a dark sedan, a rag doll flung away from the balcony to splash in the lagoon.

The two soldiers moved out. Grimaldi took the far corner of the villa while Bolan surged across the driveway and into the smoke and cordite. If an enemy groaned or moved, the soldier would drop him.

To his flank Bolan saw Grimaldi hug the edge of the building, the ace pilot trading autofire with the enemy from that direction.

Time was running out. If Calhoun had survived the 40 mm hellbomb, he would right then be scrambling for the choppers.

Clearing the four luxury vehicles in the driveway, Bolan charged forward. A bloody figure with an SMG staggered from the porch rubble. A 3-round stutter from the Executioner's M-16 sent the shadow reeling into the debris.

Cracking home a fresh 30-round magazine into his M-16, Bolan made it inside the living room. The place was reduced to piles of rubble. Stone, glass and wood shards were strewed all around Bolan. Spinning rotors vibrated the floor beneath him. Beyond the thinning smoke cloud, he spotted figures boarding the choppers through French double doors. Bolan weaved through the ruins of the living room.

Then he saw Calhoun—actually made a second of eye contact with the enemy. If the man was startled, he didn't show it.

Two Berettas in Calhoun's fists began to spit lead at Bolan. The double doors took the initial hits, glass blasting apart before the 9 mm storm swept the living room. Darting to the side, Bolan held back on the M-16's trigger, but Calhoun was already skirting away from the soldier's tracking autofire. If Grimaldi could just get out back, he could bring the helicopters down with 40 mm grenades from his M-203.

A moment later that proved a long shot.

Autofire rang out from Grimaldi's direction. It went on and on, then a figure plunged through a bay window. The guy was soaked in blood, and he clutched an Ingram, spraying lead in dying reflexes. The soldier made sure the hardman stayed down for good with a quick burst of 5.56 mm lead.

Checking his rear and flanks, finding nothing moving for his blind side, Bolan loaded the M-203. Already one chopper was lifting off.

Suddenly a deafening peal of thunder hit the ruins.

At the last instant, on the fly halfway across the living room, Bolan caught the shape bounding down the winding staircase.

One of Calhoun's men obviously wasn't going to make the flight.

The massive SPAS-12 autoshotgun began to pound out its 12-gauge barrage. The air rent asunder, Bolan barely made the cover of a toppled-over statue of a giant anaconda. There was no time to spare on trading off weapons fire. The guy was up there, blasting away for all he was worth, yelling and cursing at the top of his lungs. Stone exploded all around Bolan. Thunder echoed, and he heard boots pounding.

The Executioner glimpsed the hardman bounding off the steps, spinning to cover his retreat with his autoshotgun. He ended the enemy's run with an M-16 burst that ripped up his side, 5.56 mm lead rising up to core his skull. The killing shots and the final roar of the

SPAS-12 carried the hardman through what was left of the double doors in a detonation of glass.

Both choppers were airborne, rotor wash blowing up grit-and-glass maelstroms.

Glancing over his shoulder, Bolan saw the bloodied figure staggering on wobbly legs into the devastated opening. The soldier stopped the gunner with a 3-round stammer to the chest, flinging him back.

Outside relentless autofire shredded the night.

The choppers were already soaring over the hill, banking to angle southbound and inland. A gunman in the fuselage doorway was blazing away with his SMG. Moments later the choppers were gone, vanishing into the distance.

At the edge of a vine-covered trellis, Bolan found another of Calhoun's gunmen stretched out, his chest a bloody ruin. Grimaldi stepped into view, M-16 low, poised to fire. Apparently the dead gunman had halted Grimaldi long enough to cover the evacuation.

Side by side, vigilant for walking wounded, both men listened to the utter silence.

"YOU JUST TELL your boss we're en route and I'm looking at parking these choppers right on his front lawn. Have a nice night!"

Calhoun severed the connection with Ochoba. Cursing, he looked at the solemn or angry expressions around him in the belly of the chopper: Augustly, Sparrow and Sampson, and McBain, Kuschka and Gregor. Seething, Calhoun felt as if he could crush the handheld radio with one snap of his hand. It was all going to hell, up in smoke, unless they took charge and kicked in the teeth of anybody who got in their way. Calhoun flung the radio on a seat cushion, then sucked in a deep breath through his nose.

Beyond the windows of the Bell JetRanger, the lights of Cartagena were fading fast, giving way to the darkness of the flatland of cattle country. Should they square away the situation with Maldonado—and they would, or die where they were standing in Cali—they were returning to Cartagena, and by midmorning. Of course, he needed to get on the same page as everyone present.

The shock effect of the lightning hit had disturbed them all. He read the smoldering fires in Kuschka's dark eyes and brooding silence. McBain was chomping on a fat cigar, drilling daggers into Calhoun. Already Calhoun had taken a reaming from Kuschka about New York, the ex-KGB assassin grilling him about anything he needed to know before it hit the fan at the villa.

It could get ugly with the Russian. At least Calhoun's men were still armed and adrenalized and searching for some outlet for their rage and fear. They wanted out of this country with, of course, the load of dope. He gave them a look he knew they read as reassurance they'd get what they wanted. Even if it meant blasting their way the hell out of South America.

Still, it was incredible. The problem was in Colombia, biting at their backs. What could go wrong next?

"Remember I asked you who that guy was back in New York?"

Calhoun felt his jaw clench as he returned McBain's angry look.

"Now we're being hunted all over Colombia by an opposition we don't know squat about, nor when or where he might show up next, guns blazing," McBain rasped.

"Comrades, please," Kuschka said, raising a hand. "I

see where this is headed. This is no time for panic or squabbling among us. We will be in Cali shortly. I trust Ochoba will send word to Maldonado, Comrade Major?''

''Bad news will hit Maldonado's estate like a volcano erupting in his face,'' Calhoun said. ''I say we strong-arm this deal from here out. Here's what we know. That ship's ready to sail. It's docked, it's loaded with our stuff, bought and paid for. I don't know what the holdup is, but I say we don't take any crap from Maldonado. We let him know, point-blank, we want what's ours and we want it now.''

''I couldn't agree more,'' Kuschka said.

The strange level tone and look, and the killer's amiable demeanor, made Calhoun hesitate. If he was worried about the strike on the villa and the near lethal savaging they'd taken, Kuschka didn't show it.

A head count of their present force, and Calhoun had lost ten good fighting men. And Kuschka had lost Boris and Igor on the balcony. The problem—goddamn that guy, whoever he was—had dropped the sky on them, but Kuschka appeared confident he could deal with anything and anybody. The problem had shaved Calhoun's force considerably, and the guy would pay for it. At least Calhoun knew he had a reserve force of eight men in France, holding down their Europe command post.

''It is apparent whatever trouble you had on the mainland U.S., Comrade Major, it has followed us here. However, I believe it is to our immediate benefit that it appears this individual or individuals is not here to make arrests. To some extent that helps us in our present task. From here on, I agree with you, Comrade Major, that, yes, we will more than likely have to 'strong-arm' our way through the rest of the deal.''

McBain looked around, incredulous. "How crazy are you? We're down to a crew of nine armed men."

"Wrong, Comrade McBain. Myself, the major and you make twelve. I am sure I can convince your pilots to likewise fight if necessary."

McBain blew a smoke cloud. "What the hell are you saying? We just roll right onto Maldonado's estate and force him at gunpoint to conclude the deal and get us on our merry way out of Colombia?"

"If that is the way it has to be," Kuschka confirmed. "I have a crew in Cartagena. They are ordered to watch the German's ship. If there is trouble with Maldonado, they will board the vessel and make sure it sails. First we need to speak to Maldonado. I sense, after talking to Ochoba, that some of our product is missing."

"Listen to me. I know the man—he's stalling the deal," McBain said. "He wants more money and he's holding back some of the product. Might be as much as half. Sitting somewhere in the jungle."

"If he values his life," Kuschka warned, "that would be most unwise."

Calhoun watched McBain shake his head. He nodded at Augustly and said, "Arm the General, Mr. Augustly."

Augustly picked up an MP-5 and tossed the subgun across the cabin to McBain. The general nearly bit his stogie in two, but caught the weapon.

"It's probably been a long time, General," Calhoun said, "since you fired a weapon, much less killed a man."

Icy coldness filled Kuschka's stare and voice as he added, "But I would say this is something of an emergency, General. This is your call to duty for our organization."

"I didn't sign on for this," McBain said.

"Wrong. You sold yourself years ago, Comrade General. You sold the KGB critical intelligence on CIA operations in Eastern Europe, but that was only your beginning. You lust for money and pleasure, but I warn you, do not let your greed and your desires become our downfall. You have been promised great rewards. However, this is no time for looking toward the future. We deal with now, or there will be no future for any of us. I realize your money, your contacts inside the cartel and elsewhere have aided us greatly. However, if we lose this deal, well, I don't like to think of the consequences for all of us."

Calhoun took a seat. He heard McBain curse, but the former five-star general knew he was stuck, and in for the long haul.

Calhoun was grimly aware Colombia could indeed be the last call of duty for all of them. It would be a damn shame, he thought. They were the spine of Hydra. If they fell, there was a chance the entire Coalition could unravel and a vision of the new earth would be chalked up as just another crazy man's pipe dream.

If nothing else, at least he was on the same bloody page as Kuschka. There was hope yet.

"YOU WANT to do what?"

A call to Carlos, and the DEA special agent had arranged a private jet to whisk Bolan and Grimaldi out of Cartagena. A sixty-minute flight from a DEA airfield south of the city, and the two men now sat before Colonel Willow. The Special Forces colonel leaped up from his table after hearing what Bolan wanted.

Braced for a severe chewing out, Bolan looked around the command post. It was primitive at best. They were inside a large canvas tent, equipped with radio communications and radar screen, a computer, some tables, maps and fold-up chairs. Outside, an airstrip had been cut into the narrow forested valley a handful of miles east of the Magdalena River, about two hundred miles northeast of Cali, according to Bolan's map. There were two Apache choppers, two Black Hawks and two Lear-jets, and bivouac for the troops, as well as Land Rovers, fuel and munitions depot. Not much at all.

For all their talk on the war on drugs and hitting the problem at its source, it appeared to Bolan that Washington wasn't ready and willing to go to the mat and fork over sufficient funds to field the men and resources necessary to even put a few fingers in the dike of the narcotics dam.

Bolan stared back at the anger in Willow's blue eyes. He wanted to be sympathetic to Willow's predicament, since the colonel had been forced to bow out by orders from his superiors, have his thunder stolen. Silver haired, lean, somewhere in his early fifties, the colonel was a no-nonsense hardballer, career military, a man of honor, and Bolan knew he had seen a couple of wars, Vietnam and the Gulf. This had been the colonel's show—until the orders from on high and the arrival of Belasko and Griswald.

The Executioner was still frustrated after the latest set-back. Protocol and respect for Willow's situation were out the window. If Bolan didn't catch the scent of Calhoun soon, he would lose him again.

If Bolan's hunch was right, there were problems with the deal with Maldonado. Otherwise, Calhoun would have been gone from Colombia, not meeting with Maldonado's cronies in the first place, dancing around at McBain's villa. Further, Bolan suspected Calhoun was flying south, bound for Cali. In fact two aircraft had been picked up and confirmed by Special DEA Agent Cromman, who was still hunched and silent by the radar and radio bank.

Only minutes ago, Bolan had Cromman get him up to speed. The DEA knew that a major lab, just south along the Magdalena River and now targeted for the dawn raid, belonged to Maldonado. An informant deep inside the Maldonado cartel claimed they were working around the clock the past three days to finish turning cocaine base into cocaine hydrochloride, as much as two tons. The source said it was urgent the pickup went down that night.

Bolan could almost smell Calhoun's blood.

The Executioner had a plan, and he would stick to it. First the lab. The plan was, again, simple enough in design. According to Cromman, the DEA had a two-man surveillance team that had been sitting in the hills near an airstrip that had been slashed into the jungle. The lab was underground, with the workers pretty much a slave-labor force of local peasants. Raiding the lab itself was too risky. With all the chemicals down there, one wild shot, and everything could erupt in a fireball. And Bolan wasn't there to shed the blood of those who—whether by free choice, poverty or gunpoint—helped process the drugs.

The surveillance team had just radioed in that a cargo plane had landed. When the coke was loaded, Bolan would strike. The Executioner wanted to seize the coke and barter the load to Maldonado in exchange for Calhoun—if Calhoun was, in fact, flying to Cali to speed up his deal. Long shots and guesswork, but it was the only card Bolan had to play.

Colonel Willow rolled away from his table littered with maps, photos, overflowing ashtrays and straightened, hefting a gunbelt with holstered Beretta. "Let me get this straight. You, Agent Belasko, want me to turn over to you complete control of a raid we've planned for months on a major drug-processing lab known to belong to the latest king of kings of cocaine. You want only yourself, Agent Griswald, three of my best men—marksman, snipers—on board a Black Hawk placed at your disposal. Five men altogether, up against maybe ten to twenty of Maldonado's heavily armed best, guaranteeing a shoot-out in the middle of the night. You want transport back to Cali, then Cartagena to eventually raid a freighter we know is loaded with ten, maybe twenty tons of dope, call off the DEA in the port city, fly Griswald to a destination on hold whenever you want, and I'm supposed to stay here and sit on my hands. Tell me why I'm having a problem with this."

"It's bullshit."

Bolan turned and saw Special Agent Cromman walking out of the shadows, his lean visage hard as stone in the soft glow of light from a naked overhead bulb.

"You're damned right it is, mister," the colonel stated.

"No disrespect intended, Colonel," Cromman said, "but I wasn't about to agree with you."

The special agent had everyone's undivided attention. Cromman looked at Bolan and Grimaldi, saying, "What's bullshit is that we're down here, risking our lives to tackle something that is protected by bankers, lawyers, politicians, you name it. They make the rules and we're supposed to play. What I'm seeing here is one of those 'operations that never happened.' I've seen the Maldonados come and go. I see the death and the destruction they wreak on untold innocent lives. I think it's time a serious statement was made. However, I don't think, Agent Belasko, this is merely about Maldonado and a major load of dope. Am I right?''

"Yes—and no."

Chuckling, Cromman said, "All I ask, Belasko, is that I'm in on the hit. *If* any prisoners are taken, they could prove invaluable for ongoing DEA operations against the Maldonado cartel."

"Fair enough," Bolan replied.

A strange smile lit the colonel's eyes. He fired up a cigarette. "You know something, Cromman—I couldn't agree more with you. I just had to vent to get a feel if we're on the same page. This isn't about stealing my thunder, because I know the frustration of fighting what appears a losing battle by playing by the rules. For some time now, hell, this is damn near a dream come true. It's time to bend the rules and shove it right down the gullets of the bad guys. All right, gentlemen, you've got carte blanche. Saddle up. Whatever you need, you can have it.

"Now," the colonel growled, blowing a thick finger of smoke, "get the hell out of my face and go kick some butt."

16

True to his word, Calhoun had the choppers make Maldonado's front lawn an LZ. Disembarking with weapons ready to fire, Calhoun and the others found the drug lord waiting with an armed entourage. A dark scowl on his face, Maldonado exploded.

"You want to tell me what the meaning of this is? You want to tell me, Major Calhoun, right now, what happened to my man in New York? What the hell happened in Miami? Why is it everywhere you've gone and left men behind, there is trouble! Tell me why I should believe you have not brought me trouble to my front door! You were told to wait for my man to contact you before you made this unannounced, unwanted visit in the middle of the night. Do you want to convince me why I should even conclude this business with you people? I should have known better from the beginning to deal with men who were former CIA and KGB. All this mystery and intrigue and trouble you bring to me. You want to tell me why I am thinking that this should be our third and last deal? You want to tell me I'm wrong or completely one hundred percent fucking insane?"

Calhoun, Kuschka and McBain took front and center, all three on edge, but staying calm in the face of the drug lord's tirade. Behind, Calhoun saw his crew fan out, MP-5s and Ingrams cocked and locked. Chopper engines died and rotor wash subsided. Silence held the thick tension like a palpable force. The drug lord's gunmen, holding subguns or machine pistols, were spread out over the sprawling, manicured lawn.

Calhoun assessed the situation, but knew going in it could get ugly.

It was the first time Calhoun had been to the drug lord's hacienda-style mansion nestled in a fertile, narrow valley. Beyond the dark forested hills to the west, a distant umbrella of light glowed from the Cali skyline.

It was in Cali that Calhoun and Kuschka had originally met with associates of Maldonado's for their first deal. Once they were checked out, they met with the man himself. The first time had been three years earlier, but it seemed like only yesterday when the first shipment had left from Santa Marta for the Russian Mafia. Since then huge sums of cash had been deposited in numbered accounts all over the world. Most of the money went to the Coalition to pave the way for the new world. Whether Maldonado believed it or even cared, this was the third and final deal.

Now this, a standoff where it could all end in a moment of blind rage and treachery.

Squaring his shoulders, Calhoun looked Maldonado dead in the eye. The man was short, barefoot in white slacks, with black silk shirt. Maldonado was overweight from overindulgence, and double chinned. Five years and fifty pounds ago, Calhoun knew the man had been a vicious killer in the cartel of his predecessor, murdering and scheming his way up the pecking order. Today times were sweet for Maldonado. The bloated, squat drug king had gone soft in the body, but the savage coldness in his dark eyes revealed to Calhoun a man who wouldn't hesitate to kill again.

The man had it all, and he wasn't about to lose it, Calhoun knew. From the air Calhoun had seen the drug king owned a small private airport, a few executive jets and choppers parked near lighted hangars.

Now that he was on the estate grounds, the place was truly enormous. A twelve-foot stone wall ringed the massive compound, security cameras staggered along the top, palms and jungle vegetation growing up against the mansion. Calhoun heard rumors the man even had his own personal zoo somewhere on the grounds. He imported everything from African tigers and hippos, down to the wildlife of his native jungle. Rumor had it there was a moat of caimans somewhere on the grounds, and they were believed to have eaten more than just raw meat during Maldonado's climb to the top of the narcotics heap.

"Gentlemen," Maldonado said, and sounded an ugly laugh. "What? If I did not know better, I would think you are prepared to kill me in my own home, and even within view of my wife and children. Is that it? You want to kill me?"

As discussed Kuschka did the talking. "We did not come here for a problem. This is business, and we need to conclude our business. I have gathered from your man in Cartagena that there is a problem on your end."

"Yes, there is a huge problem. My operation in New York is now in serious danger, not to mention the disaster that has befallen me in Miami. If what I hear is true, I stand to lose billions of dollars in merchandise, men, businesses I owned! My main complex was attacked in Miami by an American fighter jet, of all things. It blew up a main hangar where I kept four tons of merchandise—not to mention I lost almost every key man I had in south Florida. Yes, there is a major problem. At the moment you are the problem. At the moment I do not have all the money I believe is due me for this most generous transaction on my part. At the moment I do not have all of your merchandise boarded on the German freighter.''

''Why is that?'' Kuschka asked.

''I have had to move several of my labs in the past week because of the DEA. I have had to reroute many of our flights from the jungle. That isn't even the beginning of my headache ever since we initiated this deal.''

''We'll take what is already loaded and be on our way.''

''Then you will be short two tons,'' Maldonado told Kuschka.

Indignant, McBain chimed in. ''Hold on a second. We've paid in full for exactly—''

''I know what you've paid for, General. After all that has happened, all the risk I have been put through, I will need more money.''

''You will get it,'' Kuschka said.

''Really. You make it sound so simple. I smell desperation on your men. I see panic and fear in your eyes. I do not like to be rushed in this manner. If you wish to wait another day, I can safely move the rest of your merchandise from the jungle to Cartagena.''

''There's no time,'' McBain said.

''Then you will get the rest of what you want when I receive the rest of my money. Or I can send a man with you to contact me wherever it is you are going. From there, my associates here can make further arrangements. In other words, I am prepared to go on good faith. If only to get you and whatever problems you are having from coming to Colombia.''

''I will agree to those terms. Now, will you make the

arrangements for us to get that ship out of Cartagena by no later than dawn?" Kuschka asked.

Maldonado seemed to think about something. "My men will show you to the guest house. You will wait there for me. I have calls to make and I believe I can arrange perhaps a delivery from one of my reserves. Maybe. No promises."

"What about the men I've bought and paid for?" Calhoun asked.

"Major, you never answered my question."

"Santiago got careless. He was followed, I don't know by who. He was killed during the gun battle."

"And you escaped unscathed."

"I got lucky."

"I hope your luck holds. Yes, the men you paid half the money for and the other half paid by Kuschka are ready to board the freighter and sail with your product. That is another matter altogether. Now that I think about it, it disturbs me. Many of these men are the best in the Colombian police and military. Some even were of great value to me over the years. Some can be replaced, others I have turned over to you for a fee I feel now is a little on the stingy side."

"They were paid well to start new lives," Calhoun said. "And to not ask questions."

Maldonado nodded. "This whole business you came to me with is most strange. Myself and my associates went to great trouble and expense to get what you wished. I do not understand it, I do not want to understand. I sense you want to hire former military men to do…what? Create a mercenary army? Are you planning on taking over Colombia?" Maldonado laughed, a sardonic sound, a vicious look in his narrowed gaze. "I have heard about what happened in New York, this army of terrorists who descended on Manhattan. I suspect, Major, you were behind it.''

Kuschka cleared his throat. ''It is not Colombia which is of interest to us. In time, Comrade, you may know. In time you may need us to come back here and offer you a new life.''

''I have everything a man could possibly want. I am the wealthiest man in all of Colombia and one of the most powerful and influential men in all of the lower Americas. I own just about every business you can imagine, I travel all over the world, enjoy everything the world has to offer, food, drink, women. I have a beautiful young wife and three children. I am revered by the masses for all I contribute to Colombia. I have fortune, and at times a fame I wish I did not have. If you think you have something I could possibly want, I ask you now what could that be?''

Calhoun watched as Kuschka showed the drug lord an ironic smile. ''I could not even begin to possibly explain what the future holds.''

''So, then you waste my time with riddles. I tell you what will not be a waste of my time. If I let you leave with that vessel and do not receive any more funds, I will be most unhappy. You could say we would never do business again.''

Calhoun watched the drug lord spin and walk away, barking orders in Spanish to his henchmen. A goon told them to follow him.

No way would Calhoun give up his weapons. Of course, if Maldonado got wind of the fiasco they had left behind in Cartagena…

He saw the others, hard-eyed with determination, pumped for the worst. If necessary, damn straight they would kill everyone on the grounds, and right in front of Maldonado's wife and kids.

OVER THE MINIMIKE attached to his radio headset, Bolan gave the orders for each man to pick a target and be ready to open fire. A moment later Cromman buzzed the soldier back.

"Hold off a second, Belasko. We've got a problem."

Through his infrared binoculars, Bolan gave the landing strip another hard search.

It was a narrow runway, carved in an arrow-straight line out of the jungle, making the coming strike tightly confined, with no margin for error. DEA intel and recon photos of the target site were on the money.

What Bolan now saw, though, upped the ante and put some of the odds back in the enemy's favor.

Whatever, it was too late to stop now.

Twenty minutes ago Grimaldi had dropped them off, north, beyond a low forested hill. The Black Hawk was now already moving in, skirting low beyond the west hills, soon to fly up from the south. But the chopper was only to be a diversion while Bolan, Cromman and the three-man sniper team struck from behind.

After the DEA surveillance team met them at the LZ and showed them the quickest and safest path to the target site, Bolan ordered them to fall behind. He wanted this wrapped up, a lightning strike, and now there was indeed a sudden problem. One look and Bolan already knew what it was.

He saw the dark shapes milling around the cargo plane. It was a de Havilland DHC-6-2000, and it was being loaded with large burlap sacks. Bolan counted eleven men armed with submachine guns near the plane, two more near the edge of the jungle. Maybe two dozen workers, men and women, moving double-time from the stygian darkness of the jungle, hauling the dope for the twin-prop plane.

And there was a woman with an AK-47. Incredibly, bucking the order whereby machismo ruled in the lower Americas, the lean black-haired woman appeared to be in charge, her voice barking orders in Spanish, most likely urging the workers to move faster. There was a chance, beyond the jungle noise of birds screeching, an occasional monkey howling and the incessant buzz of insects, someone had heard the helicopter.

Flares were lit.

Bolan then clearly saw the three figures, their hands tied behind their backs, as they were roughly pulled farther from the plane. Finally the bound shapes were forced to their knees.

"They've got my people," Cromman told Bolan. "That bastard, Maldonado. He did it. They don't look too good, either. What they'll do is use them as shields against a raid. But once they think they're clear and free, they'll kill them and ditch the bodies in the jungle. It's happened before. You copy, Belasko?"

"I copy. We move anyway. Take out the ones guarding the agents first." Punching a button to illuminate the dial of his chronometer, judging the distance from his position at the base of the forested slope, Bolan figured a dash across a stretch of about thirty yards of no-man's-land was going to make it tight, and tricky. Come up on the port side, take down the plane.

While in flight, Bolan had already laid out the attack strategy. Armed with M-16s, Cromman and the Special Forces team designated as one, two and three were already positioned inside the jungle tree line to the east, with targets lined up in their crosshairs.

"Thirty seconds," Bolan told his team, then raised Grimaldi and said, "Game time."

At first it appeared as if it would go off like clockwork. Sprinting for cover, M-16 poised, Bolan was angling for the rear of the plane when the Black Hawk veered from the far edge of the hills. Up there, Grimaldi hit the floodlights, washing a beam over the landing site that momentarily blinded and froze the enemy.

Then all hell broke loose.

As planned, Cromman and the sniper team were chugging out silent rounds. Panic hit the enemy and they started spraying wild autofire at the chopper, then realized they were being savaged from behind.

On the run, Bolan triggered his M-16 as at least a half-dozen armed shadows plunged, screaming in pain and outrage, before they lay utterly still. The Executioner reached the rear of the plane and helped take down the guards around the captured DEA agents with a 3-round burst from his M-16. It wasn't a second too soon, as the enemy was already leveling weapons on the DEA agents. One by one the falling enemy cried out in pain, tumbled, weapons blazing for the sky. An agent bowled down one gunman who then tried to rise but was crucified by a quick stitching from Bolan.

The mystery woman began to fire in all directions. She held back on the trigger of her AK-47, her frenzied spray of lead chopping up the workforce. She headed for the jungle, her arm reaching out to lock around the throat of a worker. Suddenly she released the worker and melted into the trees. Then she fired from the jungle, muzzle-flash stabbing the blackness. She was desperate, killing anything that moved, apparently hell-bent on creating as much havoc and chaos as possible, either to cover her escape or to make sure the plane took off, Bolan guessed.

Around the plane, enemy shadows held their ground, but quickly died where they stood.

The propellers on the plane were already spinning.

Racing up the starboard side, Bolan saw an armed shadow bellowing through the doorway, *"¡Vamos!"*

Bolan blew him off his feet with a 3-round burst. Hitting the doorway, flipping the selector switch to single-shot mode, the soldier saw the pilot look his way from the cockpit, then start to raise an Astra pistol. A stroke of the assault rifle's trigger, and Bolan cored a 5.56 mm message of doom through the pilot's temple before the man could get the bird rolling.

All around the landing strip, shadows were screaming, darting into the jungle. Ahead of Bolan the helicopter landed, its rotor wash adding even more noise to the sporadic rattle of autofire.

Crouched, Bolan peered into the hull of the plane. It was stripped, naturally, of its passenger seats. The hull was piled with countless burlap sacks. Nothing moved in the gloomy overhead light, but Bolan didn't trust first surveillance. Cautious, he climbed through the doorway, fanning the gloom with his M-16.

Suddenly a shadow, hollering as it rose over a pile of sacks, nearly lined up Bolan in the tracking fire of a subgun. The soldier's M-16 drilled one round between the shadow's eyes, sending the guy sprawling in a bloody spray over a sack as brief return fire spanged the doorway above Bolan.

He gave the cargo hold a thorough search. Outside all weapons fire had suddenly ceased. Moving for the cockpit, Bolan saw Cromman poke his head through the doorway.

"We're clear."

"The woman?" Bolan asked.

"Gone."

"What do you mean, 'gone'?"

"We'll search the jungle, Belasko, but unless one of us got lucky and nailed her, she'll use the jungle and escape. You can be certain any path leading to the lab is thoroughly booby-trapped. I have to wait until after dawn to go in."

"Who was she?"

"I don't know."

Bolan put her out of mind. He had the load, spotted the radio console in the rear of the aircraft. The Executioner was moving on to deal with Maldonado.

"How are your people?" Bolan asked.

"They're beaten up pretty good but they'll make it with medical attention. I've got a few bad guys out here wounded, but they'll live."

"Find one who speaks English. Find out if he can radio Maldonado and bring him here."

"So that's it, Belasko? You got what you want here, and now what?"

Bolan watched Grimaldi move up beside Cromman. "I want you to tell my pilot exactly how to get to Maldonado's estate and just what we can expect when we land this bird there."

Cromman shook his head. "You must be crazy."

"More like driven."

"Once you cut me loose, I guess this was all something that never happened."

"It happened, all right, Cromman. The worst is yet to come if I have something to say about it. That didn't happen, either."

Grimaldi was already in the plane and moving for the cockpit.

17

The first light of dawn was breaking over the Cauca Valley when Grimaldi began to make his descent. Clearing the forested mountain range, the cargo plane approached Cali from the north, then veered east. Beyond the ace pilot, Bolan glimpsed the skyline of the young city, the skyscrapers looming over the countless multicolored tiled roofs dotting the outer reaches of Cali proper. High atop a mountain the soldier caught a bird's-eye view of a statue of Christ before the commandeered aircraft came out of its bank, began dipping for the slender black ribbon of runway in the distance.

The course charted on a grid map by Cromman, from the jungle lab to the drug lord's compound, proved as accurate as any of the DEA intel Bolan had so far received. The small airport was tucked near the massive walled hacienda. A lush green landscape swept away from Maldonado's compound. Scattered across the valley, Bolan saw other smaller haciendas, most likely sugar or coffee plantations, here and there a smattering of grazing cattle. Most of the valley was still sleeping. That would soon change.

Grimaldi looked back at Bolan. Both Stony Man warriors still wore blacksuit and webbing, but were now minus the combat cosmetics. Bolan had his M-16, set on full auto, the M-203 loaded with a 40 mm grenade. Grimaldi's M-16 with M-203 was likewise combat ready.

Waiting to land, Bolan began to feel the toll on his body, suspected Grimaldi had to also be holding on with the final reserves of strength. The two men had been running on adrenaline since departing Stony Man Farm. For Bolan the hellish journey had sapped even more energy since New York. With little or no time for rest, let alone sleep, eating when they could, Bolan knew the only thing keeping them going was savage determination to bring down Calhoun and whoever else conspired with the ex-SF major. Grim resolve, combined with the long fighting experience of two warriors who had survived countless campaigns against savage and skilled opposition, would have to see them through.

And there was still the nagging puzzle of Hydra.

Little conversation had taken place between the two longtime friends. Other than ironing out the logistics and mapping out a battle strategy for each leg of the mission, Bolan and Grimaldi had hung in there in pretty much grim silence. It was pointless to ask questions when there were no clear answers so far as to the agenda of the enemy, other than a major drug transaction. All they could do was keep hunting, taking the fight to wherever the enemy could be found. It was hit-and-run all the way, but instinct warned Bolan it wouldn't end in Colombia. At the moment he wasn't even thinking beyond Maldonado.

"If our man isn't there, Striker?"

"Then we go back to the port city. Once we're back in the air, I'll radio our man in Cartagena. Touch base with the colonel. We'll need a jet fueled and ready to fly."

"In other words we're not holding out a lot of hope our target is on-site."

"There's always hope."

Bolan looked at their pawn. His name was Sanchez and fifteen minutes earlier he had used the radio to contact Maldonado. Bolan's message via Sanchez to the drug lord had been simple enough, even though it was somewhat lengthy. Before contact with the drug lord, Bolan had written out the message with pen and paper, and made Sanchez go over it until he got it right.

The frightened look in the man's dark eyes spoke volumes to Bolan. Slouched on a bench, Sanchez kept his hand over his wound. During the hit on the jungle airstrip, Sanchez had taken a bullet high in the chest. The slug had passed clean through, after shattering his collarbone. There was a lot of blood soaked into the man's jungle-camouflage shirtfront, constant pain in his eyes, but he would make it long enough for Bolan to set the stage.

"Two men are flying in to meet with you," Sanchez had said over the radio. "They have your product from the river lab. They say they have come a long way from Miami to make you a proposition. They say we will land in fifteen minutes. They say to bring no more than four men with you or they will recreate Miami."

Just as Maldonado blew up in rage, Bolan had severed the radio contact.

Of course, Bolan expected Maldonado to bring a hard-force along with him. But the plan was to get the drug lord jumping to retrieve his dope. Let the man's short fuse burn down, all the while Bolan and Grimaldi braced to ignite a storm that would end Maldonado's reign as Colombia's premier drug king.

Again it was touch and go. If Maldonado fielded a

crew of more than ten gunmen, Bolan realized they might not get airborne and make it back to the Special Forces base. If Calhoun was at Maldonado's estate, then Bolan would use the dope as leverage to draw his enemy out. He had to believe Maldonado put the life of one man as less than nothing compared to what Bolan figured was in the neighborhood of two tons worth of cocaine on board.

Now that he knew the moment of truth was approaching, Sanchez put up a front of defiance. "It is most kind of you to personally bring Señor Maldonado's cocaine to him. Two men, throwing around their big stones, against the most feared and ruthless and most powerful man in all of Colombia. He will kill you both."

"If that's true," Bolan said, "we'll have a lot of company."

Sanchez fell silent.

"How do we play it, Striker?"

"Keep it simple. Follow my lead."

"Good enough."

"I hope it is."

Bolan took a seat as the twin-prop drug plane hit the runway.

FISTING A HANDFUL of his pawn's shirt, Bolan kept Sanchez close to him. Slowly the soldier led the man away from the cargo plane. Sanchez lugged the weight of Bolan's gift to Maldonado.

The enemy was waiting. Bolan read the murderous fury in Maldonado's eyes, the drug lord's blubbery mass quivering as he tried to fight back his temper. Fuse lit, it was now just a question of assessing, baiting and executing.

The Executioner took in the scene with one sweeping

glance. They were all gathered at the south edge of the runway. A lone white hangar with two executive choppers stood on his flank, with two other hangars in the distance, at the far edge of the runway. At first it didn't appear anyone was around the closer hangar. Then Bolan spotted two figures settling beside the building. Side by side, they crouched into position with submachine guns.

Beyond the runway Maldonado stood on a grassy clearing in black shirt, white slacks, his hands behind his back. If he was toting a weapon, Bolan couldn't see it. The drug lord had brought three more gunmen than Bolan had told him to. Even still, it was expected. Maldonado didn't intend to see the two Americans leave the runway alive. The hardforce was spread out on both sides of their boss in a staggered line. They kept their weapons low by their sides. It was a hardware mix of mini-Uzis and Ingram MAC-10s.

Behind the Executioner, Grimaldi was hunkered in the doorway of the aircraft. The ace pilot had his M-16 fisted, ready to cut loose. The propellers were spinning. Evacuation, though, was far from guaranteed.

"Who are you?" Maldonado shouted. "DEA? Special Forces?"

Bolan shoved Sanchez away from him. "No."

Grunting, his face contorted in pain, Sanchez lugged the heavy burlap sack toward Maldonado.

"I have your poison, Maldonado. Your man has a sample, just to show I'm serious. I want an exchange."

"You bastards! If you are the ones who caused my disaster in Florida..."

"It's becoming a smaller world as we speak."

"Now you come here and steal from me!"

"We can fix it all here," the Executioner said, finger tightening around the M-16's trigger.

Maldonado scoffed. "And live happily ever after?"

"It's possible. I want Calhoun."

Maldonado cursed Bolan. "Give me what you stole from me, then we will discuss him."

"I don't have time to haggle. Is Calhoun on the grounds?"

Maldonado hesitated, then spit, "No. My drugs!"

Sanchez staggered up to the drug lord and dropped the sack at his feet.

"You disgust me!" Maldonado told Sanchez, then slashed a cracking backhand over the man's mouth. Sanchez dropped on his back.

A gunman opened the sack, checked its contents, then nodded at Maldonado, who said, "Kill this piece of garbage."

Bolan checked his fire as Sanchez screamed for his life. A brief stutter of gunfire, then Sanchez sprawled at Maldonado's feet.

"My drugs! Now! Or I will kill you!"

"Three men, drop their weapons and come get the load," Bolan said. "Three men! Do it, Maldonado. You've got us covered from the hangar. We're only two. What are you worried about? Push it, and my man can take care of them from here."

Maldonado erupted in blind rage. "Do not tell me what to do! You Yankee bastards are responsible for destroying my business in Miami. Is that what I'm hearing? Tell me the truth!"

"Deal with now. Where's Calhoun?"

Maldonado shrieked an oath, losing it fast. "My drugs!"

The Executioner made the judgment he knew he would before landing. "If that's your only answer..."

Without warning, Bolan opened up with his M-16. He

caught them in an instant of shock and paralysis where he got the initial jump. Sweeping the gunmen, left to right, Bolan mowed them down with a long burst of 5.56 mm lead. Two gunmen managed to open up with SMGs, but Bolan beat them to it. Enemy blood and shredded cloth took to the air. Maldonado suddenly screamed, pitched to his back.

When the hangar was vaporized a heartbeat later in a brilliant fireball, Bolan knew Grimaldi hadn't wasted any time getting into the deadly act.

As the enemy kept falling under his relentless savaging, Bolan glimpsed Maldonado clutch his leg. Apparently the drug lord had taken a wild round from one of his own.

"Bastards!"

Slowly, slapping home a fresh magazine into his M-16, Bolan rolled up on Maldonado. The drug lord was all alone. A quick search of his flanks, and Bolan found no movement from the flaming wreckage or elsewhere.

Maldonado struggled onto his knees. Hate and pain seized the man's eyes like a ravaging fire. "What do you want?"

"Calhoun. Where is he?"

"Cartagena. He's gone."

Even as Bolan felt his heart sink in frustration, he knew he had won a minor victory here, at least. One less Maldonado in the world could save untold innocent lives. Since O'Malley's death, it had never been Bolan's intention that he bring ultimate justice to Maldonado. New York, though, had merely set the table for what was becoming a baffling campaign where the unknown and the unexpected were more and more thrust at Bolan. He would take what came his way. Maldonado was on the plate.

"Listen, I have money. You want money?"

"No."

"Then what? You can't just kill me! I have a wife and children."

Bolan almost laughed at the brazenness and absurdity of that plea. The soldier wondered how many families this man had destroyed through the poison his empire created, or outright slaughtered in vengeance or to keep the good life from fleeing him through imprisonment.

"I'm sure they'll inherit the kingdom," Bolan said.

Maldonado snarled, "Why? Who are you?"

Bolan drew the .44 Magnum Desert Eagle. Maldonado's eyes widened in terror and he lunged at his adversary. The last words Maldonado heard in his savage life were, "I'm the end of the line."

18

Raw anger and frustration boiled the Executioner's blood. The black-and-white picture, taken by Carlos from a church overlooking Cardona Shipping, showed Calhoun, McBain and other unidentified players rolling through the main gate.

The ship was gone.

So was the enemy, according to Carlos, who had spotted a chopper flying west from the shipyard thirty minutes after the target vessel cast off. It stood to reason the main force of the enemy wouldn't ride with the ship.

The enemy had flown.

Bolan was far from finished with grim business.

It was well into a morning that was already eaten up with logistics and scuttling back to Cartagena for Bolan and Grimaldi. First the flight back to the Special Forces base, delivery of the late Maldonado's dope. It was a gift from Agents Belasko and Griswald for Colonel Willow and Cromman, sure to be used to set up bogus drug deals to nail future potential traffickers. From there, Grimaldi had flown Bolan to the DEA airfield in Cartagena, dropped him off for Carlos, who was waiting with the vintage Monte Carlo.

Bolan and Carlos were now on a narrow cobblestone street, parked near the shipyard.

Grimaldi had flown on, and was now on the Caribbean isle. With his handheld radio, Bolan had just radioed Grimaldi. Fire Eagle was fueled, fully armed to its twelve-ton capacity of bombs and missiles and ready to fly.

First Bolan had to deal with a few problems at the shipyard. He needed to know the final destination of the dope vessel, but that was only for starters.

The Executioner was hell-bent on sinking Calhoun's ship and sending its poison sinking to the bottom of the Caribbean.

It was a cloudless day, the sun blazing its rays like diamonds off the infinite blue expanse of the Caribbean. Bolan was going to turn this day into one of the darkest the enemy would know—up to that point. For damn sure, they would get the message, wherever they were, that he was coming after them. There was no place on earth where they could run far enough, hide deep enough, kill hard enough.

"It cast off two hours ago?" Bolan asked.

"More like two and a half."

"Okay, a ship that size, does it max out at top cruising speed of fifteen knots?"

"Something like that, give or take."

Bolan stared past the gate at the docked freighters and container ships. There was a row of warehouses, tucked up against the massive piers and pilings. Workers milled about, forklifts rolling to and from bays. No guns in sight, but Bolan knew better than to trust first glances.

"Let me guess," Bolan said. "Cardona is an associate of Maldonado."

"You got it."

"Maldonado's history," Bolan said, and quickly told the DEA special agent what happened in Cali.

Carlos showed no reaction. "Unfortunately all that does is open a void for a shooting war."

"I understand. Someone has to claim the crown."

Bolan had a mini-Uzi with attached sound suppressor in special holster beneath his loose-fitting windbreaker, the Beretta and .44 Magnum Desert Eagle likewise holstered with spare clips on his webbing for the hardware.

"Other than the big ships, what's here?" Bolan asked.

"Pleasure boats, you know, yachts, cabin cruisers."

"How about powerboats?"

"Big ones. Cigarettes, too. One other thing. Two of those powerboats slid in behind the ship fifteen minutes after it sailed. We've learned only recently what they are. We call them 'shark patrols.'"

"And?"

"In the stern they have a mounted M-60 machine gun. They haven't come up against any official military or law that's looking to board a vessel suspected of carrying dope, but there's always a first time."

"Not that you're aware of."

"Okay."

From the duffel bag, Bolan took another mini-Uzi, four clips, and handed the weapon and spare clips to Carlos.

"Are you up for what I have in mind?" Bolan asked.

Carlos gave it some grim thought. "I think the sooner I see you leave this country, the better. For the opposition, that is."

AT THE FRONT GATE, Bolan got busy. The big American was out of the Monte Carlo, the security guard rolling from the booth, when Bolan squeezed the trigger on the mini-Uzi, a whispering stream blasting out the two cameras mounted on both sides of the gate. The guard was reaching for his holstered pistol, but Bolan was all over him in the next eye blink.

The sound-suppressed muzzle dropped between the guard's eyes. Relieving the guard of his pistol and tossing it away, Bolan growled, "Do you speak English?"

"Yes."

"Do as I say and you may live to find a new job tomorrow morning. This shipyard's going out of business."

As ordered, the guard opened the gate, then Bolan threw him in the back seat of the Monte Carlo and piled in beside him. "Where do you keep the powerboats?"

"What?"

Carlos rolled past the gate. The DEA man had already told Bolan that Cardona's office was at the far north end of the pier.

"The specials, the ones that go out with certain ships, the ones with the machine guns."

The guard sputtered, "A shed. Next to Señor Cardona's office."

With no time to spare, Bolan told Carlos to step on it. Workers scattered along the dock, froze at the bay doors, guys shouting at the Monte Carlo as they were forced out of its speeding path.

The big ships blurred by the soldier, then the pleasure craft roped to pilings came into sight.

"We're here," Carlos said, jerking the vehicle to a stop in front of a building that looked little more than a large wooden shack.

Bolan dragged the guard out, told him, "Beat it."

The guard didn't have to be told twice. The soldier ordered Carlos to watch his back. Next to the office, Bolan saw the large shed, its doorways raised off the water, high enough to let the armed powerboats slide out without opening the doors.

Mini-Uzi out and poised to fire, Bolan bulldozed into the office. A beefy man dropped his phone, was rising from his desk when the Executioner zipped a silent stream of bullets into the wall above his head.

"Who are you? What is this?"

"Mr. Cardona, I assume."

"Yes!"

"I don't have time for games." Bolan flung the intel photos of the enemy on the desk. "Those men watched a ship sail a little over two hours ago. What is its final destination?"

Cardona scowled, putting some defiance into his eyes. Bolan leveled the mini-Uzi on the man's heart. "You've got two seconds."

Hesitation.

"One."

"Marseilles! I have no idea who you are or why you are interested in this ship, but you are playing a most stupid game and there are men—"

"Skip it. Your boss is dead."

The shipping man balked.

"I need one of those powerboats. You know, one of the specials. First I need you to chart out that ship's course. Do it."

Cardona sat. Bolan kept his weapon trained on the man as he rifled through a desk drawer. Cardona shoved a nautical map on the table, took a pencil and began to scribble on the chart.

Bolan lowered his weapon and was moving for Cardona to scoop up the chart when the man made his play. Whether he was ordered to fight to the death against any raid on the shipyard or was motivated by panic or terror, Bolan would never know. Cardona reached behind his back, and was whipping out a large-caliber handgun when Bolan stitched him across the chest with a stuttering zip of 9 mm Parabellum manglers. Cardona toppled over in a heap.

Bolan snatched up the map. A moment later he was outside, hastening his strides for the shed with Carlos beside him. Cautious, weapon ready, the soldier moved through the open door.

A narrow triangular pier hugged the lone powerboat. There was a tarp over a bulky object in the stern. At first glance the sleek white powerboat with its deep-V hull looked capable of hitting thirty to forty knots at top speed. To overtake the dope ship would require some time, but Bolan wanted to be on hand for the fireworks finale.

"You know how to read this?" Bolan asked Carlos, shoving the chart at him.

"Either way, it won't be hard to find the vessel. They have to go north, then cut to the east...."

"I know my geography of the region. You drive. We hit open sea, and it's full throttle."

Both men bounded into the powerboat. Bolan pulled off the tarp and found the M-60 was already belted. Behind the soldier, Carlos fired up the big V-drive engines. Bolan cast off the mooring line.

"Looks like we're topped out on fuel," Carlos said.

A quick glance at the bare cockpit and stern, and Bolan knew the boat was stripped of all necessities, built for speed and distance only.

No one came into the shed as Carlos pulled away from the pier. Whether the target vessel would be alerted by someone at the shipyard, Bolan didn't know, and didn't really care.

He was on the handheld radio as soon as they cleared the building. Fire Eagle was just about all the soldier would need.

So far, as they pushed out for open sea, it looked like smooth sailing.

In about an hour or so, the Executioner knew that was going to change.

IT WAS A MOMENT for celebration, laughs and backslapping all around.

Aboard what Kuschka had called the Russian version of the American Learjet, but capable of reaching Mach speed and holding up to thirty people, they were drinking vodka and beer, smoking cigars, cigarettes. In general, just unwinding after wrapping up the biggest and most grueling deal to date.

Calhoun took a seat in the cabin, fired up a smoke and decided to relax himself. From the wet bar he had poured a tall vodka, neat.

Beyond the portholes, the endless blue expanse of the Atlantic Ocean was a beautiful sight to Calhoun. The sky wasn't only the limit, but it was also freedom, all light and sweetness.

The future.

They were moving on, heroes, conquerors. Including Kuschka's four-man KGB crew from Cartagena, twenty fighting men were crammed into the long cabin. It was party time, even though the mood was somewhat reserved.

Looking over his shoulder, Calhoun gave Augustly a weary smile and a thumbs-up. Captain Steiner of the freighter ship *Mars* had just radioed they were well out to sea, no problems. Smooth sailing.

Next stop—Marseilles.

At the moment Calhoun didn't even want to think about the Colombian ordeal, the haggling with Maldonado, the scrambling back to Cartagena, making sure his new mercenary army and twenty tons of product were safely on board and en route, clear, sweet and free.

Goddamn, the future looked promising indeed.

If there was to have been a DEA raid or other problems, it would have happened at the shipyard.

"Have to hand it to you, Comrade," Calhoun said to Kuschka, who was enjoying a vodka himself, almost grinning over the rim. "You know how to look ahead. How long had you had that airbase outside Cartagena?"

"To succeed in life, Comrade Major, a man must cover all—how do you say?—angles."

"That's how we say it."

Even McBain, Calhoun saw, looked relaxed. Things were shaping up.

"Well, gentlemen," McBain said, raising his glass. "A toast. We've been through hell and back on this, but we're seeing daylight finally. To the Coalition, the future and the salvation of mankind as we see fit."

They were raising their glasses, laughing when the radio crackled to life.

Calhoun nearly dropped his glass when he heard Captain Steiner barking in a panic-stricken voice, "Mayday! Mayday! We've got a problem! Come in!"

In the background Calhoun heard the rattle of weapons fire, the garble of shouting and cursing. Calhoun froze.

"We are under attack! A fighter jet just blew right over our deck!"

"Fighter jet!" McBain rasped.

Calhoun felt his heart skip a beat. For a second he thought he was going to throw up.

The ship was miles away, but Calhoun could almost see the face rolling up in his mind, cold eyes set in that death mask.

The problem.

IF TIMING WAS considered everything in life, then it was certainly true of a precision military surgical strike.

The time it took for the gunboat to cut across the calm seas felt like an eternity to Bolan.

When it finally happened, the Executioner was in sync with Fire Eagle.

Locked on.

The two shark boats were tailing the big freighter when Bolan had Carlos come up on their port side. At first the two-man crews on each gunboat were uncertain of Bolan's intent, perhaps believing they were being joined by one of their own.

Before they realized what was really happening, it was too late.

Bolan hit them with a relentless fusillade of M-60 autofire. From stern to bow, the Executioner poured it on. The stream of 7.62 mm NATO lead ate up the enemy gunboats. Fiberglass, wood and flesh erupted in the deafening barrage of Bolan's man-eating lead. From the deck of the freighter, they were firing away, even as Fire Eagle made a run over the vessel.

Grimaldi skimmed the deck so low, Bolan thought he might plow into the wheelhouse.

Under the soldier's M-60 wrath, one of the gunboats erupted into an oily fireball as he hit the gas tank.

"Peel off and turn around!" Bolan told Carlos, shouting above the roar of the explosion and the growl of the powerful engine.

Bolan radioed Grimaldi and gave him the order.

Drop the sky. All of it.

Fire Eagle rolled to the west, straightened out, came around and began its final deadly run for the vessel.

Carlos swung the gunboat around, gave it full throttle and cleared ground zero. Looking in all directions beyond the white spume in the wake of the gunboat, Bolan found nothing out there but wide-open sea.

Nothing but the enemy's ship, and a dream on board to carry on its agenda.

And, of course, a solitary fighter jet, swooping down for the kill.

Grimaldi unloaded the whole twelve-ton payload. Eight missiles streaked for the hull. As the Sparrow and Sidewinders were flaming en route to obliterate the ship, Grimaldi opened up with the M-61 Vulcan, raking the ship. A series of 20 mm HE shells produced a marching line of fireballs two heartbeats before the vessel was lost forever in a gigantic explosion.

Judging by the carnage, the Executioner knew there wouldn't be even a shard left to list and sink.

Behind, Bolan heard Carlos whistle and voice an oath in awe.

"THEY'RE FIRING missiles at—"

Calhoun heard the explosions, then the captain's voice abruptly died.

Static, then nothing at all.

He was locking eyes of disbelief and horror with Kuschka, when he felt something sharp pierce his hand. He looked down, saw the blood flowing from the wounds in his palm where he had crushed the long sliver of glass.

The cabin spun in Calhoun's eyes. He bellowed in pure rage.

*The heart-stopping action continues in
Executioner #242,
the second book of*
THE HYDRA TRILOGY
*DOOMSDAY CONSPIRACY,
coming in February.*

The dawn of the Fourth Reich...

Destroyer™

#114 Failing Marks
The Fatherland Files Book III

Created by
WARREN MURPHY
and RICHARD SAPIR

From the mountains of Argentina the losers of World War II are making plans for the Fourth Reich. But when the Destroyer's brain is downloaded, he almost puts an end to the idea. Adolf Kluge plans to save the dream with a centuries-old treasure. But then, the Master of Sinanju may have different plans....

The third in The Fatherland Files, a miniseries based on a secret fascist organization's attempts to regain the glory of the Third Reich.

Available in February 1999 at your favorite retail outlet.

James Axler

OUTLANDERS™

HELLBOUND FURY

Kane and his companions find themselves catapulted into an alternate reality, a parallel universe where the course of events in history is dramatically different. What hasn't changed, however, is the tyranny wrought by the Archons on mankind...this time, with human "allies."

Book #1 in the new Lost Earth saga, a trilogy that chronicles our heroes' paths through three very different alternate realities...where the struggle against the evil Archons goes on....

THE LOST EARTH SAGA BOOK 1